SCARRED KNUCKLES

ASSA RAYMOND BAKER

GOOD 2 GO PUBLISHING

SCARRED KNUCKLES
Written by Assa Raymond Baker
Cover Design: Davida Baldwin, Odd Ball Designs
Typesetter: Mychea
ISBN: 978-1-947340-51-0
Copyright © 2020 Good2Go Publishing
Published 2020 by Good2Go Publishing
7311 W. Glass Lane • Laveen, AZ 85339
www.good2gopublishing.com
https://twitter.com/good2gobooks
G2G@good2gopublishing.com
www.facebook.com/good2gopublishing
www.instagram.com/good2gopublishing

Words from the Author

Dear Reader,

I've been told that I should take some time out to better introduce myself to you. I don't know why, but I said I'd try. Even though I love writing and telling my stories, I don't have many words when it comes to talking about myself. I'm just me. I really do love struggling with the madness to get as much of the movies playing in my head out onto paper for you to enjoy. When I'm in my writing mode, I don't look at the TV, talk on the phone, or listen to the radio until I get my first draft out on paper.

I'm sure you know by now that I'm a member of my state prison's populace, so with that said, I'm not allowed the use of computers for my craft. Yeah, I old-school it. That's why I always thank my publishing team for the work that I know they have to do to get my stories out to you. Most of the time it takes about three black ink pens, four yellow legal pads, thirty-two typing ribbons in this old outdated thing that I use, five boxes of Wyler's Iced Tea, about a pound of M&M's that I use as a serving size for a reward for every twenty-five pages I complete, and ninety to one hundred twenty days to get my stories out. Then I'm right back to working on something new.

Most of the time it's something I started in the middle of the last story. I don't know how many stories I've written since I started back in 2007, because I send them out to family for safekeeping, and many are untitled. I lost a few when my dad was called to heaven, so I gotta make up new parts to some of my stories, like in Dream's Life, which had four finished parts to it, but I can't find the rest, so I'm rewriting them.

I've gotten asked a lot about how I come up with my stories. Well, you can believe it or not, but they're based on times in my life that I dress for your enjoyment, and they're dreams that won't go away until I put them on paper. Let me see, what else I can tell you?

I was raised in Milwaukee, Wisconsin, and besides being an author, I'm a loving father to some very beautiful but weird kids. I'm a son, a big brother, and the oldest of seven, an uncle, papa, and teacher. I was married, but my wife was not. One of these days I'll tell you that story.

I'm single, but I have a best friend that I love very much. I don't think I could live very well without her, so she's my life partner.

My three favorite books to read are, first, Great Expectations by Charles Dickens. He has a girl named Estella that I like to quote: "I must be taken as I have been made. The success is not mine, the failure is not mine, but the two together make me." I like that. I also enjoy reading The Gifts of Imperfection by Brené Brown, and God's word. Without it, I wouldn't be able to find a reason to smile in this hell I live in. One day I'll give you the story about how I ended up where I am, too, so look out for it.

Well, I don't know what else I've got to say. Oh yeah, I enjoy reading your reviews of my work, so please keep leaving them. If I could, I'd respond to them all, especially the ones I get on social media for my poems. Now I gotta get back to work.

PREFACE

Approximately 128 hours had passed since Beysik came home from the hospital. He knew that in order to take the reins of his father's operation, he needed to power through his pain. So with the aid of the flashy gold Leo-headed walking stick Nyte had picked out for him, Beysik slid into the passenger seat of Rich's ruby-red Ford Mustang GT.

The young boss was curious to know who Rich had been going through to cop three kilos of soft white work needed just to keep his small part of Beysik's drug operation going. Beysik could never have an issue with Rich using the money that was left with him to keep shop open. As a true hustler, that is exactly what he was supposed to have done. The girls could not have done it, nor could Noeekwol. They would not even know where to start. So now, Beysik's issue was that the money Nyte had given him, from what Rich had been turning into the girls, did not add up; and now sitting in the soft leather seat of Rich's new whip gave him a good idea why.

"B, you sure you're up for this already? I can handle it by myself and reset it up for you to meet another time, when you're 100 percent on your feet, bro."

"Bro, let's roll. I had enough downtime. Now it's time for the boss to boss up and get back at it. If your connect is holding the way you say he is, then I'ma need him to double them three you copping just to see how it do down the way. Plus it's showing me he can handle my flip. If he can, then I ain't gotta put your bitch on the highway no time soon."

"He got that shit, bro. And don't think I missed that lil' shot you sent at me about me copping three. Come on, now, you know how I get it up, bro. We going in to snatch up five of 'em," Rich boasted, lying about the actual number of bricks he had been getting.

Unknown to Rich, Beysik had reached out to a few of his loyal clients to get an understanding of how Rich had been handling business with them. They immediately asked Beysik when was he was bouncing back in the game. They all stated that Rick had been taxing them as well as giving out garbage dope. Three of Beysik's clients informed him of the number of kilos they were buying; and collectively, just the three of them were purchasing the five bricks Rich had just claimed to be heading to pick up on the re-up. Beysik had to ask himself how Rich planned on hitting them with what they needed as well as keeping shop open for him.

"Aye, how long have you had this here?" Beysik asked about the car to change the subject.

He did not want to let on what was really on his mind.

"A lil' more than a month. I just got it from having the rims slapped on that day I ran into you at the hospital and shit," Rich answered. "Hey, did you holla at them bitches about not telling me what hospital you was in and shit? I would've came and checked on you. But they were being all funny acting and shit."

"I handled that, but what size rims is these, 24s or 6s?"

"Both, I got 24s in front and 6s in the back, so it can sit the way it do and still ride good."

When they arrived at the former furniture store, located on the northeast side of the city on the corner of Palmer and North Avenue, Rich had taken him into the heart of the ESG's hood.

The first thing that sparked Beysik's attention was that there was not one of them out on the clock. The next was the setup of the meeting place. The parking lot was fenced in, which made for one way in and one way out. Beysik was not about to let himself be caught in a death trap.

"Bro, how many times have you met with these muthafuckas here?"

"This is the first time. We usually just bust moves in traffic. But Nut had us come down here because this is a new batch, and I thought you would wanna come in and check it out first."

"Yeah, I don't like being closed in, so don't park in there. Park on the street. As a matter of fact, I'm not about all of that walking. My back's fucking with me just sitting, so I'ma chill in the car and let you handle it. I've heard of P-Nut, so I'm sure he knows me, and I know you know what I like. So, yeah, I'ma chill out here," Beysik said, staring out at the building.

"I told him you was coming with me so he wouldn't trip about it, so you good?"

"But like you said earlier, I ain't 100 percent, so I can't take no chances down in this hood. Shit, you can see if fam will come out to the car and holla at me."

When Rich got out of the car and went inside, Beysik scrambled over to the driver's seat just in case he needed to make a prompt getaway. He sat and watched Rich disappear through the service door of the building with the money bag. He then took caution to really scan the area. There was nothing moving surrounding the building, which was really strange for the east side of Milwaukee.

Beysik's wait for Rich was not too long, but when he did return to the car, he was empty-handed. He explained that he did not like the product because the work was not flaky enough for him. When Beysik inquired about the money, Rich told him that he left it with P-Nut, so he could just drop it off to him once he had the product he was used to getting.

Beysik agreed just to play along, but the whole setup of this so-called meeting that Rich was supposed to have put together seemed fishy to him. So for that reason, Beysik would not be accompanying him whenever Rich decided to re-up again later. They traded seats before Rich pulled off. As they rounded the corner, Beysik peeped out several big, black, tinted-out police SUVs trying to look incon-spicuous in the ghetto. When Rich did not comment on them and acted like he did not see them, the seasoned thug wondered how long his partner had been working for the Feds. Right then, Mercy Bondz's words popped into his son's head. "If you can't trust 'em, bury 'em. It's always a better one to fill that one's shoes."

ONE

Bright boastful digital billboard signs lit up the warm desert evening. They all were advertising Fight Night. The Arizona sands heated up even more, as one of its cities hosted the National Mixed Martial Arts Amateur Division Championships. More digital signs hung inside above the caged ring of the packed assembly hall, showing teasing slideshows of the various fighters in action on the event card. Back in the locker rooms of the arena, males and females with the heart to step inside of the locked steel cage with another all shared the same thoughts of bringing on the pain, until one of them got knocked out or tapped out from the pressure of the better fighter trying to rip off one of their body parts. All that pain would be for a chance to earn a slot in the famous UFC's octagon and the $500K cash prize. They all prayed and warmed up to do just that.

Noeekwol's thoughts were no different than his opponent's, as he lay flat on his hard six-pack abs on the floor of the makeshift locker room while getting massaged by one of his heavy-handed teammates.

Noeekwol's five foot eleven, 205-pound frame was almost without an ounce of fat on it, thanks to his conditioning and training to get him ready for the event. For him, the battles he was about to enter into tonight were the first real steps toward what he had been working toward since he first discovered how to use his hands and vicious feet effectively. Noeekwol's dream was to show his father what he was truly made of by winning and becoming the next UFC light heavyweight champion.

Noeekwol knew that in order to be that title belt holder, he would have to take it from a very well-trained animal of a man. So he trained harder than he ever had before. He was in the gym five to eight hours a day, five days a week. And when he wasn't hard at work in the gym, he was at home shadowboxing to perfect his striking. Noeekwol was highly skilled in boxing, which was his first love, and grappling, which was his second. He always pushed himself harder so he would always be the monster in the cage when that bell rang.

A hard knock on the locker-room door by the security team informed him that the last match was about to be over and that he was up next. The monster got up on his feet, threw a few fast jabs into the air, and then gave his team the okay to have them key up his hype and walkout music. Once Noeekwol heard the pounding bass of Yo Gotti's hit song "Act Right," he began his bouncy dancing stroll out toward the ring.

♫ I'm going going back back to the Bay,
Rest in peace Mac Dre.
All I do is talk yay,
In the club got them bottles on replay.
Tryna break a record like a DJ... ♫

Noeekwol sung along while the official looked him over outside of the cage. His gloves and mouth guard were first cleared, and then the ring official applied pure petroleum jelly to

Noeekwol's face before allowing him to enter the ring with the awaiting challenger.

"Who's ready for some light heavyweight knock-out action? If you're ready, let me hear you say KO!" the announcer said, hyping an already hyped-up crowd. "Fighting! Out of Milwaukee, Wisconsin, with a mixed martial arts record of fourteen wins and no loses. Introducing Nooeeeekwol Bondzzz!"

Noeekwol heard his name and then slowly and dramatically entered the center of the ring. He was dressed in his signature black and gold trunks with TEAM CHOSEN in bold white letters written across his butt. His opponent for the first three rounds of the night's events was a big Latino brawler with a record of nineteen wins and two losses who called himself "La Drello" ("the Brick"), because of his enormous fists and block head. As soon as the announcer handed over control of the fighters to the referee to begin the action, Noeekwol went into his zone and blocked out the huge, excitedly roaring fans.

"Round one!"

The Brick raised his hands as he charged in on Noeekwol while looking to take him down to the mat for some of his signature ground-and-pound work. But Noeekwol was ready for him. He dodged the first advance and pushed him away and picked a sweet spot for when the Brick tried the move again. And after just a few testing jabs later, the brawler charged at him once again; only this time, Noeekwol did not push him away but introduced the Brick's face to a vicious hard combination of fists. This slowed the Brick all the way down and bloodied his battle-scarred face. Without letting up, Noeekwol delivered three hard knees that crushed his nose and knocked his untamed opponent out cold. The shocked referee quickly dove in between him and the shattered, unconscious La Drello before Noeekwol could do any more damage.

Noeekwol snapped out of his kill zone and thrust his arms high above his head as the fans went wild with cheers and applause. There was no question as to who the winner of this first-round knockout was as the medics rushed in to tend to the Brick.

TWO

Two assassins with a very personal agenda on their hardened hearts posted up outside of the busy Milwaukee casino waiting for their target to show his face. Approximately an hour after they confirmed that the man they were looking for was indeed inside the building, he showed his predatory face.

"Look up! It's game time," Slim announced, perking up in the driver's seat of their Buick while watching Mercy and his wife, Felisha, emerge arm in arm through the big shiny brass-and-glass exit doors.

"Yep, I see 'em," Fame responded, tightening his grip on his gun. He was also watching the target and his wife climb inside of a clean Cadillac Escalade that the casino's eager valet had waiting idly at the curb.

When the couple was on the move, Slim took off after them, staying a few cars lengths behind as he stalked his prey. Mercy Bondz drove the scenic route through the boulevards of the city. He excitedly talked about the money he had won in bets on the amateur MMA fights that he watched on the large screens in the lounge area of the casino.

"Noe is moving up in the world. He just might be able to get to the UFC soon, especially if he keeps winning like he did tonight. Man, did you see how fast my boy punished that big Spanish muthafucka in that first fight?"

"I did. My fuckin' heart almost stopped when that big ugly-ass dude ran at my baby."

Felisha shook her head in disgust for the brutal sport their son loved so much.

"But when Noe-Noe kicked his ass, I felt sorry that boy." She giggled. "How much did he get paid for that fight?"

"Nawl, baby girl, it don't work like that with these fights that Noe is down there in. These fights are a last-man-standing type of deal."

"Last man standing? What is that supposed to mean?"

"It means he gotta beat all of the other fighters' asses in his weight class who won their fights tonight to get paid," Mercy Bondz explained as he loosened his grip on the polished wood of the steering wheel. "I believe he said he's going to have to fight three or four fights altogether."

"So after he beats all of their asses like he did the first guy's, how much does he get?"

"Is that all you think about, woman?" Mercy Bondz exclaimed, not wanting to tell his wife about the large $500,000 purse or the $150,000 bonus Noeekwol had to split down the middle with him.

"No, but it helps keep me together every time my baby gets in them damn cage fights that you talked him into doing," she said, pouting as she glared at him.

"See, there you go. I didn't talk that boy into nothing. I just give him the guidance and push he needs from time to time. And, Lisha, you're the one who put him in them self-defense classes in the first place. So don't hate on a pimp, because I wanna see what I paid for all them damn years." He chuckled.

"I ain't hatin', but pimping our son ain't one of your, as you call them, investments," Felisha said as she turned toward him and put her back against the door as she continued telling Mercy Bondz about himself as a father. "Noe-Noe can get killed in that thing or fuckin' crippled!"

"Bitch, first lower your fuckin' voice!" he checked her, pointing his cubby finger in her face. "Any muthafuckin' body can be killed at any time, doing anything and everything. That boy can be killed just walking down the street, and I can't be worrying about that. I can't control that shit. But what I can control is how he lives the life I gave him. Lisha, it was my money that bought all of that pricey-ass equipment that your babying ass wanted for him back when you put him in them classes."

"It was for his safety."

"He would've been just as safe if you got that shit from Play It Again Sports. So he is an investment that I'm allowing to keep over 50 percent of his winnings," he slipped up and told her, wishing he could take it back as soon as he did.

"Really, Mercy! How about I start buying your shit from the Goodwill and see how you like it?"

She could not help herself from laughing at the thought of her husband in anything low fashion or used.

"Ha ha, you're funny."

"So if you get 30 percent of his money, that means I get 50 percent of yours, since he's half mine and it was my idea to put him in the classes. If that's not reason enough for you, let me throw in that I'm your wife?"

"Girl, you lucky your pussy's too good to share with your big-head ass," he told her, pulling over and parking in front of their modest suburban south-side home.

"Ummmm, show me it's good to you, daddy," Felisha said as she pulled him into a passionate kiss, knowing that it would get deeper once she got him started.

They were making out in the front seat of the big SUV, like they used to do when they were young lovers, when suddenly the window on Felisha's side imploded and sprayed her with bits of broken glass. She screamed loudly when she saw a shadowy figure reach through. It grabbed her and snatched her over to the opening by her shirt sleeve. Before Mercy Bondz could make a move for the gun that he kept between the seats, he was shot in the hip through his door.

Fame was not shooting to kill. He was just letting Mercy know not to make any sudden moves until Slim was through with him.

"Agggghhh!" Mercy cried out in pain, quickly abandoning his idea of going for the weapon. "You can have it all, just please don't hurt my wife!" he pleaded, holding Felisha's hand tightly while putting pressure on his wound.

"So this is your bottom bitch, huh?" Slim exclaimed, hitting her in her pretty face with a hard backhand. "I thought your punk ass only liked young hoes."

Fame snatched open the driver's door and demanded all of the cash the pimp had on him right there, because he did not trust walking either of them into the house. Fame was sure that a nice amount of cash and jewelry could be found in there to cover the personal job he was on for Slim's family, but robbing people wasn't really his thing, so he let it go.

"Here, take it and just go. That's over fifteen Gs. Y'all can have this truck, too. Just let us go!" Mercy Bondz pleaded.

"Nawl, I don't want your truck!" Slim barked before he reached over and caressed Felisha's bruised cheek while flashing Mercy a deceitful grin. "I want you to know how it feels to have someone you love taken from you!" he told him before shooting Felisha in front of him. Her warm blood splattered onto Mercy's face. "That's for taking my lil' cousins! Bitch!" Slim told him, and then pressed his gun to Felisha's head and pulled the trigger, putting her out of her pain.

Fame saw that his friend was not in his right mind, so he quickly pumped two bullets into Mercy's chest. He then fled the scene, but not before Fame caught movement in one of the home's windows. Unknowingly, they were being watched by someone in the Bondz home after Fame's very first gunshot.

THREE

As always, before going out for the evening, Felisha had gone over the emergency contact instructions with her part-time playthang and loyal live-in nanny, Heaven. Heaven was also one of Mercy Bondz's working girls. Even though Heaven had not once sold her body for the pimp, she still belonged to him. The young whore was saved from the streets because Felisha took a liking to her the very first day she laid eyes on her. Even more so, after finding out that Heaven was drug-free, except for smoking a blunt or two here and there, Felisha told her husband she wanted Heaven to help her out around the house and with the children. It was always whatever Felisha wanted, she got with the seasoned pimp. So Mercy Bondz agreed and made Heaven their live-in nanny.

After putting the little ones down in bed for the night, Heaven quickly warmed herself up two big slices of pizza and rushed back into the family room to finish watching Noeekwol's matches on the 65-inch HDTV that hung nicely over the polished stone gas fireplace. She curled up in the corner of the velvet La-Z-Boy sofa with her pizza leftovers in one hand and a cold wine cooler in the other. She smiled when she heard his signature hype music by Yo Gotti begin playing for the third time that evening. Heaven had watched Noeekwol win his first two fights with lightning-quick knockouts. She knew that if Noeekwol won his last match he would be crowned the new light heavyweight champ and have a shot at fighting in the Ultimate Fighter Champions' steel cage.

Just like the two matches before, an official checked him over and then gave him the okay to enter the ring. The guy he was fighting was much bigger than the others.

"Oooh, hell no! That punk looks like he eats weights for fuckin' dinner!" Heaven said aloud to the TV.

She did not believe the big European opponent was only seven pounds heavier than Noeekwol because the two were the same height. She figured they were trying to cheat with him.

Heaven sat on the edge of her seat watching Noeekwol stand toe to toe in the center of the ring in an all-out slugfest with the big man known as the Viking.

Then suddenly they tied up, both bleeding and both trying to get a break in the last few seconds of the clock. The bell rang, ending the first round. Heaven dashed out of the room and into the kitchen for another wine cooler and another slice of pizza, just in case. She made it back in front of the TV just as round two began.

Noeekwol was chopping on the Viking's legs with hard leg kicks. Heaven knew the kicks would have broken down anyone else, but the Viking was still standing and trading jabs with Noeekwol while looking to take it to the floor. When Noeekwol went for a high round-house head kick, he slipped, lost his footing, and slammed to the floor hard. The Viking dove on top of him, but Noeekwol somehow managed to keep the big man in half-guard. They stayed down wrestling for better position. The Viking was tired, so much so that he made the mistake of easing up when he heard the tap of the two-minute warning. That was when he suddenly found himself in a savage armbar.

Heaven cheered as Noeekwol cranked on the arm with all he had in him, trying to make his opponent tap. He was about to give up when the Viking roared out in pain while simultaneously patting him on the shoulder. The referee rushed over and forced Noeekwol to let go of the man's arm and declare that the match was over by tap out.

Heaven screamed with joy. She was happy for Noeekwol, when all of a sudden she heard screams followed by gunfire coming from right outside the house. She felt something was wrong, so she dropped to the floor and crawled over to the front window, just in time to witness two men standing outside of Mercy Bondz's Escalade with guns pointed inside.

* * *

Social media friends were in a hot gossiping hysteria because sometime in the early morning hours, a well-known pimp and nightclub owner, along with his wife, a self-proclaimed same-sex rights activist, were murdered. Mercy and Felisha Bondz were found shot to death inside of their fancy Cadillac parked right in front of their home. The breaking news reports on the television showed all of the neighbors standing out on the surrounding lawns and sidewalks intrigued as they watched the police secure the appalling crime scene. The Bondz family's humble six-bedroom, single-family home and SUV were almost surrounded on all sides by the bright flashing lights of the MPD squad vehicles, EMS forensics vans, and a bunch of TV news media crews. The busy area had been blocked off by yards of cold yellow police warning crime scene tape.

The execution-style homicide of the couple was now the fastest high-profile murder case in the city of Milwaukee, and the media liked nothing more than a violent murder mystery to follow. Besides, Mercy Bondz was the perfect victim to gossip about. The nightclub owner's true identity was well known in the hoods. Mercy Bondz was a heartless pimp that used his nightclub as a front for his real business, which was sex-trafficking mostly sexy, curious teens. The pimp's only kryptonite was his wife and bottom bitch. She was a sexy, quick-witted Angie Stone look-a-like with a major in business and the mother of his children. Mercy Bondz had fathered approximately ten children with a host of different young women, but the ones he had with Felisha he cherished the most because of her. She was the only woman who had ever truly stood up to Mercy, which is how she became his wife.

They left behind a son, Noeekwol, age twenty-four, and two daughters, ages nine and seven. And Mercy had another son, Beysik, age twenty-one, whose mother took her own life after she found out that he had married Felisha instead of her.

FOUR

Noeekwol proudly wore his well-deserved light heavyweight belts over his shoulders as he broke away from his own victory celebration to have a private party with an exotic blond Asian woman. The champ had the sexy ring girl believing she had been his lucky charm. The ring girl had given Noeekwol a congratulatory hug and kiss on the cheek after winning his first match.

As soon as they stepped out of the building, he powered on his phone and was immediately flooded with a rush of missed calls, alerts, and text messages, many of which delivered the tragic news of his parents' murders. The champ was so distraught by the news that he got into an Uber and left the beauty at the casino's curb feeling confused and self-conscious. Noeekwol returned Heaven's calls and then made arrangements for the next flight back to Milwaukee.

* * *

Detective Tabitha Allison had just finished writing the last of her homicide case report when she was called out to the Bondz homicide scene. Tabitha Allison was an athletically built, Emily Blunt look-a-like in her early thirties. The detective was only running on three hours of sleep after the previous case that she and her absent partner, Morton Sadd, had just closed. Tabitha was starting to feel the effects of her sleep deprivation when her new commanding officer, Chief Ludwig, arrived on the scene. She knew he would be waiting on her to give him something to make himself look good. The commander needed some information to feed the people when he did his press conference. The media address was specifically done for those in the city who did not believe that black lives mattered to the police. All lives mattered to Chief Ludwig, and he was not going to take these murders lightly.

Tabitha did her on-scene inspection of the two victims' bodies as they were found in the Cadillac. She took down detailed notes before allowing the forensics team to take photographs of the couple. The team then removed the Bondzes from inside the SUV to be photographed once again before they were hauled away to be autopsied. When the bodies were moved, the detective did a more thorough inspection of the Escalade, hoping to find something that could help shed light on what had taken place at the time of the ambush.

She next interviewed the neighbors who called in the shooting to 911. She started with the ones who had the best view of the SUV from their bedroom windows.

"You're late!" Detective Allison barked at her partner when he finally decided to show up at the crime scene.

"Hey, I got here as fast as I felt I needed to be here!" Detective Sadd shot back at her, not liking the grumpiness he heard in Allison's voice.

Detective Sadd reminded most people at first glance of the comedic actor Jack Black. He was almost forty-five years old and had been a MOD detective for two months shy of fifteen years.

"What?"

"I made a pit stop at the station to try to catch you there; and to my bad luck, you had gotten called out already," he lied when he caught up to her.

"Sadd, what the fuck do you have a cell phone for if you never read your text messages? I sent you three texts telling you about this call and that I was already here."

"I said I was sorry. Now can you please just drop it and fill me in on what we got here? I don't know how your man deals with all of your damn complaining," he said after flipping open a small leather-bound notepad as he prepared to jot down what she told him about the crime scene.

"Fuck you!" She frowned, storming off toward the Cadillac.

"Really, Allison? Are you being serious right now?"

Sadd did his best to stay in step with her. Tabitha stopped in her tracks and took a couple quick calming breaths before addressing Detective Sadd again. They had only been partners for about four months, and, so far, she hated working with him.

"You missed two dead bodies: one male, the other female. Both shot while sitting inside the Caddy over there," she explained as she pointed to the SUV that was being loaded onto a flatbed. "They're believed to have been married, and both lived there."

Allison pointed once again, this time at the house where a couple of uniformed officers were walking in and out, across the street from where the two of them were standing.

"Wait. What did you say the vics' names were?" he asked, with his dark blue eyes focused on the Cadillac Escalade sitting on twinkling gold-tipped chrome 26-inch rims.

"Markee and Felisha Lee Bondz," she answered without having to look at her notes.

"Mercy fucking Bondz!" he exclaimed excitedly. "I thought I recognized that Caddy from somewhere," he said with a smile. "So he finally got his ticket punched, that old piece of shit!"

"Okay, it's good to know how you really feel, but I said Markee, not Mercy."

"Yeah, I'm thinking they are one in the same because that fancy whore sled over there belongs to Mercy Bondz."

"Okay! Good, you know one of the vics. So that should make my job a little bit easier," she added as she pulled out her pen and pad. "Tell me everything you can remember about him."

"Well, one of our vics is a pimp that went by the name of Mercy Bondz. I know the Feds have been trying to bust him on human trafficking charges for about a year now—maybe longer. I know he has a son that I really believe we need to locate and get off the streets right away, if we don't want to be picking up any more bodies anytime soon."

"Do you got a name for the son so we can put out a warrant for him? If not, we can get it from someone inside the house."

"Nope. Damn! I can't . . . I can't think of it right now," Sadd responded, frowning as he racked his brain to remember. "But Allison, in my defense, it's a really weird one. I wrote it down at the time, but this is a new notebook."

"It's okay. Let's just get it when we do the interviews with the family members inside."

"Wait, you didn't do that first?"

"I saved that for last, because I was waiting for you!" she shot at him before she marched off in the direction of the house.

Once they were inside the Bondz family home, the detectives met Heaven, and she gave them two names before she stopped talking and shut down. The name of her boss's eldest son was the first one, and the second was the name of the family lawyer. She made sure the detectives understood that she knew her rights and was not allowed to continue talking to them without either of them present. Heaven then asked them to leave the house until one or both of the men she had mentioned made it to the house.

"What the hell was that? I'm not going to just fucking sit waiting outside until some sleazebag lawyer gets here or that asshole son returns from fucking Arizona!" Sadd exclaimed when they got outside. "She has our cards. We can come back later! Come on, Allison, you know I'm right. And it looks like you're moving like a zombie right now because you're so tired."

"Okay, when you're right, you're right!" she conceded with a telling yawn. "I'll call in the warrant for the son and then call it a night and go home."

"No, Supergirl, you've done enough here. I was the last one late to the scene, so it's only right I handle the rest. Go home and get some Zs. I will call you as soon as he's in custody and not before."

"Morton, the only way I'm going to agree to that is if you can tell me the name she gave us," she said, waiting with a silly grin on her face for him to answer.

"His name?" he repeated, fishing out his notebook from his pocket. "I got it right here," he retorted while quickly scanning the pages. "Noeekwol Bondz," he said softly, and then again louder for her. "This name doesn't ring a bell, but I got it. So, there, are you happy?"

"No! Not so fast. Spell it for me please?"

"Are you being serious right now? Come on, I just read it off to you from my notes. Don't you think I had to spell it to write it? I mean, I had to graduate some schools, too, to get this job," he joked.

"Yeah, I don't know. I'm still in the air about that. I may need to see your diploma," Allison shot back while still grinning. "Partner, what I want to know is how you spelled it."

She already knew he was not paying attention when she asked Heaven to spell the son's name for them. Sadd was too busy checking out one of TMJ 4's female news reporter's ass as she did her job in front of the camera.

"I'm not going to play with you on this, Allison. Either you go home, or you can stay here. I'm done being Mr. Nice Guy."

"Sadd, I'm not playing with you on this. I know you spelled it the way you learned to in school at an early age long, long ago. I did the same at first, but I had to think about the type of flashy narcissistic father you described our vic as being. So I asked just to be sure. Now please write this down so there won't be any issues with the arrest warrant," Detective Allison explained, and then paused to give him a moment to find his pen. "N-O-E-E-K-W-O-L! It's almost spelled the way it's pronounced."

"No shit. That's some good junior detective work!" Sadd said, surprised by her thoroughness but also impressed. "I got this. Good night, partner."

Tabitha didn't even look back at her stubborn good-for-nothing partner as she climbed behind the wheel of her car and headed home. She silently prayed that he did not mess up, because she really did need to get this case closed ASAP so she could catch up on some much-needed rest and relaxation.

Forty-five minutes later the truly exhausted workaholic was dragging herself through her kitchen door. Tabitha headed straight on into her bedroom, where she was happy to find her boyfriend, Bret, of almost four years asleep in bed.

Any other night, Tabitha would be stripping out of her clothes while waking up Sean with a hot slutty blowjob so he could make her cum until she passed out. But not this time. Tabitha was trying her best not to wake him. But Sean opened his eyes as soon as her butt touched the bed after her quick shower.

"Ummm, hey!" he groaned, reaching out for her.

"Hey yourself," she said before giving him a brief peck on the lips. "I didn't mean to wake you. Go back to sleep." She yawned.

"Hon, you look beat. Just get yourself comfortable, and I'll be right back with what you need."

Sean was up and out of the room before she could think to protest. A short time later he returned with a plate containing two microwaved ham, egg, and cheese English muffins in one hand and a glass of orange juice in the other.

"Here! Just eat what you can. It'll help you sleep better."

"You know I love you, right?"

She gave him a real kiss before wolfing down one of the breakfast muffins and all of the cold juice. When Tabitha's head hit the soft memory foam pillow, the last thing she remembered before falling off into dreamland was Sean's arm draped over her bare slim waist.

FIVE

Beysik Bondz was crossing the southern Indiana state border alone in a shiny black Mazda Miata hardtop convertible with the top up. He had just swapped cars with his cocaine connect's driver in the small town just before the border. Beysik would not usually be the one making the trip. But since the only two people that he trusted to do it were out of state at the time the call came in, he decided to make the trek himself. Beysik connected his phone to the radio and pulled up his playlist, because the quiet car was making him feel extra paranoid.

The young thug relaxed a bit and cranked up the radio when his father's new favorite song, "7 Years Old," by Lukas Graham came on.

♪ Once I was 7 years old,
My mama told me
Go make yourself some friends
Or you'll be lonely.
Once I was 7 years old . . . ♪

Beysik sang along, and the touching lyrics always made him think of his mother before she took her own life. Unlike the words of the song, when he was a young boy, his mother told him always to watch closely the ones who called themselves his friends.

♫ *It was a big, big world,*
But we thought we were bigger
Pushing each other to the limits.
We were learning quicker,
By eleven smoking herb
and drinking burning liquor
Never rich so we were out to make
That steady figure . . . ♫

Beysik did not remember much about his birth mother, but he did remember her words and how she was always on her hustle. Passion had always gone out of her way for Mercy Bondz and her son. Beysik knew it was his mother's way of showing them her love.

♬ *Once I was eleven years old,*
My daddy told me
Go get yourself a wife
Or you'll be lonely.
Once I was eleven years old . . . ♬

When Beysik went to live with his daddy and Felisha, the truly heartbroken pimp told him to make money off his wife and marry the game because "whore money is for-sure money." Beysik took in all of what he was told and applied it to his young life. Now twenty years old he was in love with the dope game. He learned that hoe money was slow money and came with too much stress. But the ten thousand grams of soft white blocks in the trunk were fast and for-sure cash.

"I only see my goals, and I don't believe in failure!" he sang before replaying the song as he crossed the Wisconsin border.

Beysik let the music envelop him as he floated down the highway toward his exit. He took Three Mile Road when he got off the highway, all the way to the safety of the stash house that he kept in a cozy apartment building in Racine.

The first thing he did when he walked inside the stuffy, muggy apartment was turn on the TV so he could watch the replay of his big brother's fights. Beysik had set the DVR before he left, but he forgot to turn on the air conditioner, and now the warm place was unwelcoming. Not wanting to power through the heat, Beysik tossed the duffel bag of drugs into the safe that he had hidden in the back of the closet. He then walked back outside the apartment to give it time to cool off, as well as to pick up a few things from the store and something to smoke.

SIX

Noeekwol stood apprehensively in the baggage claim area of the crowded airport, looking for his bags to come around. His anxiety had him feeling a bit suffocated and irritated by the others that were also standing in front of the carousel. He dreaded what he had rushed back to Milwaukee to face, especially at a time when he should be enjoying the shine of his hard-earned accomplishment just hours before.

The champ kept telling himself his parents were not dead. It was just Heaven misunderstanding what was really going on, or his mother just trying to get him home sooner so she could celebrate with him. But then Heaven's very distraught voice kept replaying in his mind.

"Noe, you gotta get here. You gotta come home now! Somebody killed Pops and Mama right in front of the house!"

"Bitch, don't play with me like that!"

"I'm not, Noe! I'm telling the truth. I was watching your fights when I heard the shooting. I was scared to look out the window at first, but something didn't seem right. So I looked and I seen 'em. Noe, I can't! Just please get here now!" Heaven begged.

"Shut up! I'm on my way. You know what to do, Heaven. Don't talk to nobody, and don't let nobody talk to the kids either. Call Jake and tell him I said for him to come over there right now. And don't go nowhere until I get there!" he instructed her before ending the call and trying his parents' cell phones with no luck.

Noeekwol was retrieving his bags when he suddenly got the feeling he was being watched. His mother had always told him to trust his gut when he did not have anything or no one else to trust, so he did. As he turned to scan the faces, a trio of TSA and MPD officers quickly app-roached and surrounded him.

"Noeekwol Bondz?" the MPD officer asked, stopping in front of him.

Noeekwol knew that if he was asking, he already knew who he was. Further, his name and face were just plastered on the sports channels and news sites everywhere because of his new status in the world of MMA. So the champ did not attempt to hide his identity from them, and since he had not done anything wrong, he guessed they were there to escort him to his parents' house.

"Yeah, that's me! What's up, Officers?" he answered clearly.

"I have a warrant for your arrest. Please drop your bags and turn around slowly," the officer exclaimed, with his hand resting near his gun.

"Whoa, wait! I ain't done shit! I don't have any warrants. Y'all must be misunderstanding something here," he explained, dropping the bags like he was told.

Before he could turn around, they were all over him. At first, Noeekwol continued to try to explain, but he shut up quickly when one of the TSA officers drew his gun and pointed it in Noeekwol's face.

"Don't make me do it, champ!" the officer pled with his gun slightly shaking in his hand.

Noeekwol dropped his head and held his breath as they slapped the cold, plastic, black handcuffs tightly around his wrists. From that moment on, he did not have any doubt in his mind that the call that he had received from Heaven was real.

"So you won all of your matches, huh? Looking at you right now, one couldn't tell," the MPD officer said, trying to make small talk.

"Yeah, just think of what them other guys' faces look like right about now," another officer said to his friend before he turned back to Noeekwol. "I bet you weren't expecting a welcome home party like this, were you, champ?"

Noeekwol said nothing. He just allowed them to parade him through the busy airport. While walking, he thought of all of the most gangster scenarios his dad may have gone out in. From the way he was being treated at the moment, he just knew his parents had gone out in an all-out gun war with the Feds or the MPD SWAT team.

He suddenly found himself being shoved inside the back of a black-and-white squad car by the officer escorting him. Without another word, the champ was hauled away to the Downtown Milwaukee police station.

Once they had him there, he was instantly fingerprinted and tossed alone inside a surprisingly clean cell. With nothing to do but wait for his lawyer, Noeekwol lay his sore body on the hard, unmade rubber mattress and closed his eyes. He knew he would not be able to sleep, but he just did not want to stalk the cell's window.

SEVEN

Sometime around mid-afternoon, Tabitha was snapped out of her sleep. Her annoying co-worker was relentlessly ringing her phone while simultaneously pounding on her front door like a nutcase. Sadd did all of this to wake her up and get her out of bed.

"Yeah! What do you want, Sadd?" she snapped, throwing the warm plush covers off of her. "Are you at my home right now banging on my door?" Tabitha inquired, noticing that the pounding had stopped when she answered the phone.

"Yeah, it's me, so don't shoot," he chuckled. "It's time to rise and shine. Our boys picked up Mr. N. Bondz two hours or so ago. Now, Allison, before you start bitching about needing your beauty rest, you've slept for six hours, and if you throw on a little eye shadow, I promise no one would be the wiser," he teased and laughed.

"Sadd, answer this honestly. Does anyone in your life really like you?"

She ended the call without allowing him to answer.

Just like any other day of the week, Bret was already up and gone. Tabitha knew he had already left bright and early because he left her a sweet note on the bathroom door. It read for her to text him when she found it, and he wished her a safe day at work. He closed the note with a smiley face and a heart he had drawn. She texted him like he had asked her to, while she prepared to take a shower just to make her partner suffer and wait.

More or less than 30 minutes after hanging up on Sadd, Tabitha rushed out of the house with a breakfast sandwich between her teeth. She held a case file and a banana smoothie in one hand and used the other to lock up the place.

"What? Nothing for me?" Sadd asked, looking up from some hot female profile pictures that he used to pass the time when he had to sit around.

"Just drive and let me eat in peace, please!" she begged as she took a big bite out of the egg, ham, and cheese muffin.

"Pushy, pushy!" He smirked, putting the car in gear and pulling into traffic. Sadd filled in Tabitha on what he had been up to while she was sleeping. "Would you believe the Bondz kid is a champion MMA fighter?"

"That's interesting. Do you think that and the homicides could be linked somehow?" Tabitha inquired, wondering what made Sadd tell her that bit of information about Noeekwol.

"I really hadn't thought about it. The guys at the station are all excited about having him there. I wonder if I can get him to give me his autograph on a confession when we talk to him, so we can close this shit case. This is one of those cases where the world is a better place without the pimp formerly known as Mercy Bondz."

Just two and a half hours earlier, Detective Sadd had returned to the scene of the double murder to do some looking around. All that was left for him to see were chalk circles of where a few spent shell casings had fallen, and discarded strips of crime scene tape. But the reason for Sadd going back was to see if he could persuade Heaven into talking to him. But all he received was the repeated words she had told him the first time before slamming the door in his face. The trip was not a total waste of time, because he did get a look at another female that was not around on his first visit.

"Try telling that to those children that just lost their mom and dad. Better yet, repeat that to Noeekwol Bondz and see how that works out for you," Tabitha retorted.

It did not take the detectives long to drive to work, but the Bondz's family attorney had beaten them to the station by half an hour. They found out quickly that he had been busy. The lawyer had gotten the small traffic tickets that Noeekwol was detained on dropped, and paid the $1,000 fine, which was the only thing needed to have him released. So until the release paperwork could be processed, the lawyer had the champ moved to a conference room so he could stall time. It was also a good way of keeping the detectives from questioning his client.

Jake Sharps was shiftiness in the flesh. Many people thought he reminded them of a gay Judge Joe Brown, all dressed in an expensive, flamboyant, plum-colored three-piece suit.

As soon as the detectives eyed him, they knew he was not going to allow Noeekwol to give them the interview for which they had hoped. An hour after receiving the all-clear call to take the champ home, the lawyer and his client emerged from the safety of the conference room and attempted to make their way toward the exit.

"We would like to ask Mr. Bondz a few questions," Allison stated, blocking their path through the hallway, with her angry partner by her side.

"I'm sorry, but my client is too upset from the loss of his parents to talk right now," Sharps responded in a polite tone. "I'm sure the two of you understand in your line of work how extremely difficult times like these are, even without having to sit in jail on a silly arrest warrant. While in need of medical assistance, I may add."

"Bondz, you do know we are trying to catch your parents' killers, right?" Sadd asked, ignoring the undertone of threat from the lawyer as well as his instruction not to talk to Noeekwol.

"Please don't address my client. As a matter of fact, please do not return to his home. It's my understanding that you've collected all of the evidence and have had it removed from the scene in front of the home. So the next time you want to speak to any of my clients at that residence, you will need a warrant," Sharps explained while pretending to be reviewing a legal file that he was holding as a scare tactic.

"Okay, how about you tell us where your client was at the time of the homicides?" Sadd asked before getting in the lawyer's face and trying his best to let him know that he did not frighten him nor did he like him.

"That's simple, Detective. All you have to do is pull up any sports news media source you like, and you'll have your answer while seeing him become the new light heavyweight champion."

"I'm sure there are no cell phones allowed inside the ring. So can you tell us how your client here learned of the shooting so soon?" Tabitha asked, just to back up her partner.

"I'm pretty sure you were given that answer when you interviewed my other client at the home, but I'll play along. Mr. Bondz was sent a text from a family friend who is staying at his parents' home. That friend was at the home babysitting at the time of the shooting. He then directed the friend to call me and not to talk to anyone until I arrived. Since you had him arrested at the airport, you already know how he got here as well as the time of his arrival."

"Both of his parents are dead, and the person or persons who did it are still out there somewhere. Doesn't he have any questions for us about their case?" Tabitha asked in disbelief.

She really could not believe the way the interview was going.

"My client knows if you had anything worth saying, you would be saying it now instead of trying to question him," Sharps answered using a more serious tone of voice. "Now unless you two have something to say about the suspect or suspects, or if either of you would like me to go against Mr. Bondz's wishes and file a harassment grievance with the judge, please move! My client has some arrangements to take care of."

All the two frustrated detectives could do was step aside and watch them stroll out of the building.

"Shifty punk!" Tabitha mumbled while shaking her head and biting her lip the way she did when she got upset or was thinking really hard.

"I'm thinking asshole, but what you said works too."

"I don't understand why he won't talk to us when we're trying to help him," she exclaimed as she followed Sadd back to their work stations.

"It's like I told you, that whole family is bad news waiting to happen. They will die by the code of the streets before they help us to help them."

"That's just fucking crazy!"

"Tell me about it. I'm going to look into the family some more. I am 50 percent sure that's not the same Bondz kid that I crossed paths with in the past. I'm also going to look into that Arizona stay. I wanna know exactly what time he checked in and out of his hotel and who was there with him. The punk might've hired someone there to take out his old man, so he could take over the family business or get from under Mercy's thumb—or both."

"What about the mother?"

"She was in the wrong place at the wrong time."

"I know you don't really believe that he could do something as cold as that, do you?"

"My dear partner, there's a lot of cash involved in this case that needs to be looked at. Sex trafficking is a very lucrative gig, and Mercy Bondz was very good at his job."

"I have a friend in the FBI. I'll reach out to her and see if she can tell us anything about their investigation now that their number one suspect is dead. There shouldn't be any issues for them to disclose that information," Tabitha stated before heading over to her side of their work station.

Their station was just two cluttered metal desks that had been pushed together so the detectives faced each other while they worked. It was the chief's way of building better work relations on his teams.

EIGHT

Exasperated and heartbroken, Noeekwol stood under the beaming sun at the edge of his parents' property line, just staring at the spot where they lost their lives. Heaven watched him for a long ten minutes before getting up the nerve to say something.

"Noe! Noe!" she yelled as she reached out and grabbed the hand of the man for whom she secretly held a school-girl crush. Belonging to his parents made it forbidden for her really even to converse with him without permission from his jealous and controlling father. "You need to come in the house before them police come and take pictures of you or the dirty sons of bitches that took 'em from us come back and try to get you."

Heaven's heart skipped when Noeekwol intertwined his thick fingers with hers. To most it was nothing, but to her it felt like she had been kissed by the prince. She did her best to push down her lust for him as she towed him inside the house. Heaven briefly had a flash of herself being carried into her bedroom and tossed on the bed by him.

"Where are the kids and everybody?" he inquired when his younger siblings did not come running when he entered the house.

"Aunt Tasha came and took them as soon as she saw on the news what happened. I tried to tell her you would be mad about her taking them, because you told me to watch them until you got here. But she told me she was your aunt and to stay in my place and took them anyway," she explained before she braced herself to be slapped or worse.

"That's good Auntie took 'em. It's best that they're not around here anyway; plus, she can be the one to explain to them what's going on," he said with the sadness loud and clear in his deep voice. "Aww, fuck! I left my food in Jake's car."

"Oh, do you want me to cook you something?"

"Nawl, just get me the keys to one of the cars so we can get outta here for a few and get something to eat."

"You want me to come with you? I mean, do you want me to put on something else to leave out of this house with you in?" she slightly stuttered with surprise.

Noeekwol looked at the way the leggings she was wearing hugged her curves. He noticed for the first time how good Heaven looked without makeup on and with her hair pulled back into a simple ponytail. Something emotional sparked between them. It was like he was seeing her for the very first time as a woman and not a servant.

"No, you good. We're just gonna go grab something from a drive-through and then maybe just ride around. I need to think of my next move in all of this," he said while looking at his feet.

Heaven was a little disappointed that he did not want her to get dolled up for him, but she was super excited that he was taking her out with him. What she feared most in all of what was going on was being thrown back out on the streets. This time she would be in a city that she did not really know.

Heaven's mother had kicked her out of her home in Gary, Indiana, just before her seventeenth birthday. It was right after Heaven had told her that her stepdad had forced her to suck him off because he had come home and seen her alone in her room with her gay friend, Malik, lying across the bed.

Heaven's dope-head mother took her boyfriend Cory's word when they had confronted him. He flipped it, saying Heaven had tried to seduce and blackmail him for money to get her hair and nails done. Knowing that was all her daughter had been talking about that week, the dick-whipped mother kicked her out. That was three years ago.

Young, broke, and alone, Heaven started dancing at a hole-in-the-wall strip joint in Fort Wayne, Indiana, that did not care that she was not of age, as long as she shook her tight ass on their stage. That was where she met another dancer named Nitemare. After she told Nitemare her about her story, Nitemare brought the young girl back with her to Milwaukee and into the Mercy Bondz family. That was eight months ago. Heaven was glad Felisha took claim of her before Mercy Bondz could put her to work on the streets or in one of his underground brothels.

Now that Mercy and Felisha were gone, Heaven had to come up with a plan and show Noeekwol that he still needed her around. She would do anything not to go back to that life or a worse one.

"Can I drive?" she asked after choosing Felisha's Volvo.

Her car choice was not because it was his mother's, but because she was in love with the car and always dreamed of owning one.

"That might be a good idea, because my head is all over the place right now. So, yeah, take us to get food from wherever except Taco Bell."

"Yeah, yeah! I already know that you don't like it. I was thinking more like Wendy's," she suggested, remembering how many times she had seen him come over to the house with a Wendy's cold drink in his hand.

"That's fine. We need to stop by my crib so I can grab my heat just in case," he said, following her out to the garage.

Noeekwol wondered if she could feel his eyes on her perfect behind. Heaven's walk was mesmerizing, so much so that it made him forget about his pains for a hot moment.

"Noe, have you heard from Bey at all?" Heaven inquired about his brother who had yet to show up or get in touch with anybody yet, as far as she knew.

She did not know why Beysik entered her mind while she was maneuvering her dream car joyously through the street. She was trying to make the best of her pretend date with the handsome prince of her deceased proprietors.

"No, but I ain't even turned on my phones yet," he admitted, picking up his two cell phones and powering them up. "I can't believe this shit is really real myself, and honestly, I don't know how to tell him this shit. Bey was way closer to Pop than I was," he admitted, sounding a bit sad by the acknowledgment of his relationship with his father. "Don't trip, I'll do it before we get outta this car."

"Okay, but don't rush yourself. I understand that you got a lot of stuff on your mind. I tried him myself, but he ain't got back with me. Noe, you should know that Mama always told me you are the only one who could hold things together if anything was ever to happen to Pops. So I trust you to do what's right. I'm here for you however you need me to be."

"Thanks! That's good to know."

"Oh, when we get back to the house, I got something to give you.

Mama said for me to get it in case of emergencies."

"What is it?"

"I'm not sure. I never looked inside the box. Mama just showed me where she kept it."

This was the first lie Heaven had told him. The truth is that after the police cleared out the night before, she had gone and opened Felisha's lockbox. She found cash and a journal inside.

Heaven's first thought was to take the cash and run, but she could not just run out and leave the two little ones in the home alone at a time like that. But then Felisha's sister came over and took them with her, so now the only reason Heaven didn't leave was because she didn't know where to go. And a little part of her wanted to see Noeekwol. She wanted to see if he would take her with him instead of letting his little brother take her. It would be a nightmare if Beysik got ahold of her. She felt sorry for the other girls that worked for Mercy Bondz. So for her assurance, Heaven took over half the money that was inside the box and stashed it somewhere outside the house, just so she could get to it if she needed to make a break for it.

"Alright, don't forget. You got me curious now. There might be something in it that can be helpful. Ah, damn, man! I ain't never had to plan a funeral!" He dropped his head against the window in frustration. "Man, this shit is fucked up!"

"I know. Me neither, but I'll do what I can to help. Maybe you can get your aunt Tasha to do it since she wants to be all bossy and shit."

"Yeah, Heav, you're right. You're just full of good ideas today, ain't you? I'm glad you didn't just take off with as much shit as you could carry, like any one of those other bitches on his team would have."

"Noe, I hope you can really see that I'm not like them other bitches either. I didn't have to sell myself for Pops. All I had to do was stay loyal, keep the house, and help take care of the kids. You know Mama was thinking about opening up a daycare and letting me run it because I'm so good with kids," she said proudly.

"Is that something you wanna do?" he asked while looking over at her.

"I don't know. I wouldn't mind it, I guess. Hell, as long as I don't gotta go back to shaking my ass for strangers in a crusty-ass club of fuck for my money, I'm with it," she answered before she instantly wondered if she should have been so honest with her feelings on the subject. "But I know my place. If you want me to do what I gotta do to help out, I will."

Noeekwol noticed that she sounded broken when she said that. He just watched her as she turned into the parking lot of his building and swung the car into the visitor's parking spot. She was just imitating what she had witnessed his mother do whenever they came by his place. All of the times Heaven had been over to his place, she had never once been any further than the parking lot.

"Heaven, I'm sorry. I meant to tell you just to take us to pick up the food then come here, but then we got to talking good, and I forgot too. See, I told you my mind was all over the place," he said with a smile.

"It's okay. It's been a long time since I've been able to do something like this." She then backed the car out of the space. "I think you're maybe still a little punch-drunk from all of your wins last night too," she joked.

"Punch-drunk?"

"Yeah, you look puffy and tired right now. Noe, I don't know what is so special about the gun you got over here, but it's guns at the house that you can use to keep us safe," she reminded him. "We should just go back there after we get the food, so I can give you a nice relaxing bath in the whirlpool. Let me take care of you so you can take care of us?"

"Again, you're right. I do need to soak my body and take a bath so I can get outta this jail shit!" he agreed. "Okay, ma, you got this. Show me how you can take care of me while I try to get my head together. As much as it can be together, anyway," he added, brushing a single strand of hair away from her eye.

Little did he know the feeling of his finger on her face sent a shockwave down her body. For a moment, Heaven thought about pulling over in an alley and hopping into his lap. Then she wondered how she could be so in the mood for sex at a time like this, and that thought was what kept her foot on the gas.

NINE

On the way back to the police station after their meeting with an FBI friend, Detectives Allison and Sadd made a pit stop at Subway to eat. They discussed the details of the case between consuming a six-inch spicy Italian sub, a small bag of plain chips, and two rainbow chocolate chip cookies apiece. Tabitha smiled to herself as she wondered why her partner had a diet soda. She guessed it was to humor his guilt, because he took a sip of it after every bite he took.

With the needy chief hot on their captain's ass about the high rate of gun-related homicides in the city, the captain happily passed it down to the two of them. He was pressing them to have someone charged with the double homicide before their forty-eight-hour window of success had closed. Tabitha knew she had to put the rest of the time they had to good use.

She admitted to herself that Heaven directly calling the family lawyer after calling for help, then refusing to talk to them until he was by her side, was a good reason for her partner's suspicions. If Noeekwol Bondz had nothing to hide, then why not allow himself to be questioned, and why was he not more anxious to find out who had killed his parents?

"Sadd, I've been giving some thought to what you said about the son having his father killed to take over the family business."

"Okay, yeah, and?"

"The way the parents were shot. Well, from what I remember off the top of my head, it suggests more rage to me. But I will need to see the vics' bodies again to be sure. I was pretty tired when I first looked at them," she admitted, waving her cookie as she spoke.

"Well, you're in luck," he said looking up from his phone. "I've just received a text from Amee giving us the okay to come down and inspect the bodies. That's another thing I had done while you were sleeping. I called ahead and asked to be informed when they were done with the bodies and before they sent in their official report."

"Great! You drive. I'm too stuffed." She grinned as they got up from the table to leave.

Tabitha texted back and forth with her boyfriend on the drive over to the morgue. Bret was being strange all of a sudden. He texted and asked her what time she thought she would be home, whereas he would usually just text and say he would be there waiting when she got off work. Tabitha wondered if he was about to propose and if she was ready for it.

"I'm not surprised. There's just so much violence in this city."

"Don't start, Bret!"

"When are you going to give us moving out of here some real thought, Tabitha?"

"Where is this suddenly coming from, Bret?"

"It's not sudden. You just keep avoiding it. So when?"

"Okay, since you wanna do this, I'm not leaving my job or my career, especially to keep shacking up with someone I'm not married to in a new place."

"Let's talk later when you get home. I love you!"

"You too."

"Is there trouble in paradise?" Sadd asked while parking in front of the city morgue's entrance.

"Why would you think that?"

"I'm a detective just like you are, and I've been doing my job so much longer. I'm good at detecting things, like when you replied more quickly to the texts. That told me you didn't like what was being said. Look, I know I'm a little rough around the edges, but I have a good ear and some pretty wise words," Sadd offered before climbing out of their unmarked, gold detective car and then holding open the entrance door to the morgue for her.

* * *

Back inside of his parents' home, Noeekwol allowed himself to get absorbed in the moment of emotional vulnerability with Heaven. He liked her because he could talk to her in a way he could not talk to almost anyone else. Heaven was sharp-minded and had good common sense, and she knew a lot about MMA, which was a plus. If she did not know about something, she was not afraid to ask or point out a few of his bonehead moves that she had seen him make in his last match.

"Where are you originally from?" Noeekwol asked after taking a bite of his fries.

"I'm originally from Haiti. My dad still lives there, I think. I never met him, at least not that I can remember anyway."

"Where's your mother?"

"Uhhh, my mother," she said as she rolled her eyes. But he could see more sadness in them than anger. "She's around somewhere in the game."

"The game?" Noeekwol could see some new emotion in her lovely eyes. "Are you talking about the dope game or the pimp game?"

"Hell, it's kinda both of 'em fucking with her ass."

"I can see that you don't really wanna talk about her, so just ask me something."

"Okay! Have you ever been to Vegas?"

"Only to fight. I don't like it there because there's too much going on. I leave that busy world to Beysik."

"Damn." She smiled. "There goes my plan of not taking you down in the room."

"Huh, what was that?"

"Nothing, I'm just being silly." She giggled. "Hurry up with that last bite so I can give you the bath I promised you I would."

"No rush. I like talking to you, unless you plan on getting in with me."

"I like talking to you too," Heaven answered as she allowed her truth to slip out in that moment. "I guess we can continue to have our stimulating conversation while you soak in there."

When she tried to get up from the sofa, he grabbed her by the arm, letting his hand slide down her slim forearm. He then clutched her wrist and pulled her close, until her lips touched his in a kiss. Heaven did not resist; instead, she gave in and briefly kissed him back before she stopped.

"Do you like me like that, or did I just over-step?" he asked while looking into her eyes while still holding her wrist.

She did not know how to answer, because his lips on hers made her light-headed with lust. She eased her arm free, not wanting to say anything until she was out of reach to calm herself down.

"I gotta go make your bath," she replied before she rushed out of the room.

Noeekwol was confused. He wondered if he misunderstood what she wanted from him and read too far into things. He then thought about how she told him that she had been treated by men in the past, and he shook his head at his carelessness. He tossed the last of his meal onto the table, and then went to apologize for kissing her. His plan was to blame it on grief, but in truth, he knew grief had nothing to do with it.

TEN

Loud cheers and rap music boomed from a 42-inch HDTV in front of a bunch of Milwaukee's finest, including the captain. They all watched the new light heavyweight in action, paying close attention to how he won his title. Detective Sadd told everyone he was watching Noeekwol's fights as part of his homicide investigation, since he had never seen the Bondz kid fight before. So they all joined in to help him understand what he was looking at.

Tabitha just smiled and shook her head at her commanding officer and co-workers from her desk. She could see the action on the screen through the conference room's window from her seat, and she secretly enjoyed watching Noeekwol fight.

As the final match began, just like in Noeekwol's previous two matches, the ring official did his pre-fight checks and then gave him the okay to enter the cage. Noeekwol's opponent was a monster that called himself the Viking, and to Tabitha, it looked like his only joy in life was to mangle the lesser men of the world. There was no way the officials could believe the man was a light heavyweight fighter. He looked every pound of his 250 pounds, which made him a heavyweight fighter. Tabitha knew this because she had looked up the pound amounts of each weight class as soon as she had seen the previews of the fighters.

She was on the edge of her seat watching as Noeekwol and the Viking rushed to the center of the ring and entered into an all-out slugfest. Now Tabitha understood why his face looked the way it did when she saw him at the station. Noeekwol was much faster than his opponent, so he was landing heavy fists, some of which had opened up cuts on the Viking's face. But they both were bloody messes within minutes.

The Viking looked worse but still came on strong. When he could not take any more punishment, he grabbed Noeekwol and held on to him to get a little break. They stayed tied up until the bell ended the first round. That was when Tabitha received some information she had been waiting on via email.

She collected her things and left the station to get on with her job, leaving Sadd behind watching the rest of the match. He had been right about there being another Bondz son with a unique name. This one's name was Beysik Bondz, and he was currently being held in the Racine County Jail on a petty marijuana possession charge. She knew the charge would not hold him there long, so she shot down there as quickly as she could. Tabitha was glad she made it before the Bondz family lawyer did and bailed him out while keeping him from talking like he had done with Noeekwol.

"What the fuck am I really being kept in here for?" Beysik demanded before he was seated at an interview table.

"You're a detective, so don't try and tell me it's for them two funky-ass sacks of weed that I had on me."

"You're here with me for questioning. I don't care what the county has on you," Tabitha answered, pulling out the chair and sitting across from him.

"Questions? I got one for you! Where the fuck is my lawyer?"

"I'm sure someone is trying to reach him, Mr. Bondz. I just wanna talk."

"What the fuck ever!" he growled. "Bitch, go do your muthafuckin' job and get my damn lawyer!"

"Whoa, Bondz! There's no reason for you to get belligerent with me. I don't work here. I just came down here to talk to you about your whereabouts last night."

"Yeah, I'ma have my lawyer sue all y'all asses for keeping me in here like this, with no outside contact, and after I clearly said I want my lawyer."

"Who's your lawyer? I'll call him myself, because you're right!" she said, doing her best to get Beysik to relax a little.

The detective knew she had to get him to trust her if she wanted to get any of her questions answered.

"Jake Sharps. I know they ain't called him, because there's no way he would let me sit here, especially for something so petty as having a little slut smoke."

"I know Jake, and I'll call him for you. Can you tell me where you were last night before your arrest?"

"Not without a lawyer."

"Why? Do you have something to hide?" Tabitha leaned forward in her seat. "Look here, Bondz, I came all the way from Milwaukee to talk to you. So please drop the tough-guy crap. I don't care about what they picked you up for or who you got it from!"

"Can I get some water?"

"Water?"

Tabitha got up and left the room. She could see Beysik was nervous about something, and it was not the weed he had been caught with. Tabitha found the break room and got a cold bottle of water and brought it back.

"See, Mr. Bondz, I do what I say. I told them to call Jake, and I got you your water."

"Thanks, but you said you was gonna call him yourself," he reminded her as he opened up the bottle and took a slurp.

"I did, and I got his voicemail, so I passed on his number and asked one of the other officers to keep trying to reach him for me," she lied.

She did not call Jake Sharps herself, but she did pass his card to an officer, and she asked him to call Beysik's attorney.

"Bondz, I'd like to see you out of here today, so let's stop making this so damned hard. Just tell me what I wanna know, please."

"What's so important about last night?"

"Something I can put an even longer hold on you for, if we don't have this conversation about where you were last night," she retorted before she took a moment to study the young man across from her.

Beysik was a good-looking guy, Tabitha had to admit. Even though he was in his early twenties, she saw a bit of wisdom in his hazel-brown eyes. He wore his hair in long, thin, red-tipped dreads that he had tied back at the moment. He also wore a mean scowl on his clean-shaven face. The detective also took notice that he was dressed in top-designer-brand clothing. Everything he had on looked new. There was not even a scuff mark on his Gucci boots.

"I'll say this. If you weren't in Milwaukee, you don't have anything to worry about from me."

From the way Beysik was acting, Tabitha didn't believe he knew about his parents, or he was a really good actor that missed his calling.

"I wasn't in Milwaukee. I was in Chicago with a couple of broads. We were at a little sports bar watching my brother fight for the title. After that we came back up here and chilled. I spent the rest of the night at their crib. I was on my way back there from the gas station when I got pulled over and locked up."

"Who are these broads you say you were with?"

"Shit, all I know is the one I was chilling with was named Nyte. I wasn't into her friend like that," he lied.

The truth was the girl named Nyte was his girl, and she was out breaking in a few new track whores for him and his dad. Beysik also knew that she knew what to say if anyone ever called her about him, so he was not worried.

"You're telling me that you took two women out of state and back, and you don't know anything else about them?"

"Hey, I was just trying to fuck the bitches, not love 'em, so there ain't no reason to get to know 'em like that."

"Do you remember the name of the sports bar?"

"Big Willie's, I think. It was my first time there."

"Is Noeekwol Bondz the brother you were watching fight on the TV at the sports bar last night?"

"Yeah, why you ask?"

"I watched his highlights earlier. He's really good," she honestly answered. "Okay, I got one more question. When was the last time you saw or talked to Markee? No, I'm sorry, Mercy and Felisha Bondz?"

"That's my pops and mom, why?"

"Just answer the question, please."

"I don't fuck with my pops like that, so it's been awhile," he lied. "But I spoke to my mom yesterday afternoon—around one thirty or so. Now why you wanna know about them? What kinda detective is you?"

"Homicide. Mr. Bondz, I'm sorry to be the one to inform you of this, but both of your parents were killed last night. They were found outside of their home inside their SUV, by their babysitter."

"Nawl! Nawl! What the fuck! How? I mean by who?"

"That's what I'm here trying to find out, but they both were shot at a pretty close range. So if there's anything you can think of or anyone who might've wanted them dead, please tell me so I can look into them. Help me find the ones who did this to your family," she pled.

"Nawl, man! I'm done talking. I want my lawyer now!" Beysik demanded, his eyes now narrow with a new flame in them.

"Thank you for talking with me. Again, I'm sorry for your loss. I'm going to see to it that your charge is dropped and that you are released right away," she promised him before leaving him alone in the room.

Tabitha did not leave right away. She stood around and watched Beysik's reactions on the monitor outside the interview room. She witnessed the grieving man pick up the water bottle and slam it to the floor. He then dropped his head on the table. What she saw was enough for her to believe that Beysik was not the one who had pulled the trigger that killed his parents. The detective also felt that once he was free, he would not stop until he got his deadly revenge on anyone involved with his parents' murders. She decided right then to keep a watch on him, with hopes that he could help her catch the killer.

ELEVEN

Noeekwol stood at the bathroom door watching Heaven fill the tub with steaming hot water and soothing bath salts. He could not help but notice her plump ass when she bent over to test the water's temperature with her hand.

"Heaven?"

"It's almost ready, so you can start getting undressed. I hope you're not a shy guy," she said, now facing him with a cute little smirk on her face.

"No, I'm not. Not shy at all," he said with a grin as he began to undress right where he stood with his eyes locked on hers.

Heaven's body temperature slowly rose as she watched him pull his shirt over his head to reveal his firm broad chest, shoulders, and big arms. She wanted to kiss her way down his tight abs and have herself a mouthful of what was pressing to be free from his jeans.

Noeekwol knew she wanted a show, so he gave her one by slowly unbuttoning his pants and letting them drop off of his hips while he kicked off his shoes. Once he had them off, he slipped out of the jeans and then his form-fitting boxer briefs.

"Now it's your turn. I want you to get in there with me. No, I want you to want to get in there with me," he said after taking a few slow steps toward her.

Heaven did not hesitate one second. She removed her top and exposed her firm breasts, flat-toned belly, slim waist, and wide hips. She peeled off the tight leggings, inch by inch, down her nice shapely legs. Once naked, Heaven turned off the water and turned on the jets, and then stepped inside the tub. Noeekwol followed, and then his lips found hers like before; only this time, her tongue slipped between them into his mouth, which willed him to press her further.

He sat back and pulled her with him without breaking their kiss. Noe could feel her body tremble as his hands slid down her frame. So he pulled her closer and gripped her ass, and Heaven almost purred when he broke their kiss and then sucked her erect nipple into his mouth. With her butt cupped in his big hands, Noeekwol lifted her up and lowered her down until his hardness filled her inch by heavenly inch.

Heaven was cumming from the excitement of living out one of her fantasies with a man as fine as the one she was with. The ecstasy of Noeekwol's full length buried inside her wetness was too much for her at first. She began working her honey muscles, clenching his thickness as he began to rock her back and forth slowly. She took over and worked him in and out of her. Heaven rode him hard and wild.

With the powerful massaging jets pulsating against their bodies, their moans filled the air, and Heaven rode him harder and faster. Noeekwol soon released himself in her. Heaven knew it and sped up even more until she burst. She locked her nails into his shoulders as Noeekwol dragged her orgasm out of her. All either of them could do was hold on to each other tightly. Both felt like they were a perfect match.

"Damn, girl!" he said in a low, husky voice.

"I told you that I was here for you however you need me, and I'm not leaving you."

"Good! Because I'm not through with you," he promised her, kissing her again and making her melt all over again.

TWELVE

When Detective Allison returned to Milwaukee from her interview with the Bondzes' real bad seed, she headed home instead of going right to the station. The little spat that she had with Bret via text messaging kind of disturbed her. Little spats like the one earlier had been on the rise between them lately, and Tabitha wondered why. It did not help that lately she had the feeling that their relationship was nearing some kind of a cross-roads.

Bret was forever talking about living the rich dream of a retirement lifestyle with the large inheritance that had been left to him by his very wealthy deceased grandparents. Tabitha noticed that in all of his planning, there was never mention of marriage and all of the things that come with it. She had been working hard to get where she was now on the police force, and she was far from ready to give it up for love, especially without the promise of a ring and children in the near future.

So with her stolen bit of free time, the detective planned to have a serious face-to–face, heart-to-heart talk with the man she loved so much. But how much did she really love him? she wondered as she drove home.

Bret was great looking, kind, and caring. He did not mind doing things that were considered unmanly to some, like the time he surprised her with a his-and-her day-spa date. Bret evened her out, which is why they worked and they were right for each other.

But from time to time, Tabitha craved to be tossed around and have her ass slapped in the heat of some spur-of-the-moment beastly sex. It was the kind of sex she knew someone like the young thug she had just visited in the Racine County Jail would give her. There was something about being called bitch by him that had turned her on, but she would never cross that line with a known criminal.

Tabitha's mind continued to wander as she drove. When she was just a few blocks away from her place, her cell phone rang. She quickly scooped it up, feeling a little guilty for her thoughts. She glanced at the caller ID on the screen before answering.

"Detective Allison," she stated to her partner on the other end of the call.

"Allison, I've been looking all over for you. Where are you?" Sadd inquired with a hint of excitement in his voice.

"I'm on my way to my place for a sec. I have something I need to deal with real quick, and then I'll be right there," she answered honestly, knowing that all Sadd had to do was pull up the unmarked car's GPS tracker to know where she had been and was going now. "But if what you're calling about is urgent, my matter can wait," she told him after pulling out of traffic to talk.

"Urgent? I'll let you be the judge of that. I've been married twice, so I know how personal matters can affect a person on the job. Allison, if you need time."

"I got a few things going on, which is the reason for this call," she exclaimed while ignoring his prying.

"Well, partner, while you're out playing house, the ballistics report came in. They got a match on the slugs pulled from the wife's body to ones in an open homicide case down in

Racine. I've already put in a request to have a look at their case files."

"How long have you had this info exactly? I just left Racine County lockup; and if I had known, I could have picked them up while I was there."

"Allison, I've only had this info for maybe ten minute or so. But exactly why were you down there, or is that a part of your personal matter?"

"No, it was not a part of it. I was there on official police business," Tabitha said as she rolled her eyes at his questioning. "As much as I hate to say it, you were right about there being another one of Mercy and Felisha Bondz's boys out there with an unusual name."

"Okay, what is his name and what does it have to do with what I just said? I hope it's something good, because right now it's looking like a real major break in our case."

"His name's Beysik, and it's spelled B-E-Y-S-I-K and not B-A-S-I-C," she teased. "I hope you're writing this down, or you're going to have to wait for my shift report to get it again."

"Yeah, yeah, Beysik! That's that little asshole's name that I had a run-in with a while back. How did you find him, and how come you're just telling me? Allison, I would have loved to have interviewed that jerk-off."

From the tone of Sadd's voice, Tabitha felt there was something more to that run-in her partner said he had with this family. If she wanted to know what it was, she knew she would have to play nice-nice with Sadd to get it.

"I did my job as a detective working a high-profile double homicide case while you were so-called reviewing Noeekwol's whereabouts one round after another and match after match, I'm sure," she answered, not willing to play nice at the time.

"Ha, ha! Hey, you're a funny gal." Sadd chuckled. "FYI, reviewing those matches was very educational in building my suspected profile of the champ."

"You're so full of it right now." She could not help but laugh with him. "Anyway, I put out an APB for him; and when I got an email that he was being held at the jail, I went to have a chat with him. Since he was in lockup, I didn't feel the need to disturb you to come back me up with the interview."

"Allison, you should have told me where you were going. We are partners for a reason."

"Yeah, well, you should have thought of that before you ignored my text last night," Tabitha retorted. "Hey, you said the slugs from the mother were a match. What about the ones from Mercy?"

"No matches found as of yet; and, yes, the slugs were from a different caliber handgun."

"So it confirms that there were two shooters and not just one."

"And the prize goes to Allison for her amazing detective work connecting the dots!" he teased.

"What the fuck ever!" she said as she rolled her eyes again.

"How did the interview with him go?"

"It's safe to say he didn't do it, so we can just rule him out."

"Rule him out! From what I remember of the punk, he's the type of money-hungry asswipe that would do something like kill his parents to get rich quick."

"The guy didn't even know he had been made an orphan until I'd informed him of their murders. I took a moment and watched how hard he took the news. He broke down when the weight of it fully processed for him. So, yeah, I'm sure he's not our man."

"I don't buy that. I want to have a go at him myself. What charges are they holding him on?"

"None now! I had him released from the petty drug offense that he would've never been taken in for if it wasn't for the APB that I put out for him."

"You did what? Allison, that fucking guy just played you. What you saw was his sorrow that his mother got caught up in the hit he put in motion. Or maybe he was there and was hoping she pulled through. Whatever, I just can't believe you let him go," he snapped.

"Well, believe it! I stand by my decision, and like I said to you at the start of the call, I have something to take care of right now. Please know that we're going to re-visit this conversation when I get back there."

Tabitha ended the call and pulled back into traffic. She was irritated by the way Sadd had spoken to her, and even more so that he did not have faith in the way she did her job. She really did not like him.

When Tabitha pulled up to her place, Bret's car was not there, so instead of calling him to the house to talk, she turned the car around and headed to the station. She repeatedly counted backward from twenty-five, just the way she had learned in the anger management class she had been ordered to take as a uniformed officer for breaking a suspect's fingers.

Tabitha stomped through the police station and headed straight over to her work station where Sadd was sitting on the edge of his desk eating donuts and talking with a flirtatious female officer. Tabitha was about to confront her partner about the way he had spoken to her on the phone, when the captain suddenly appeared.

"Sadd! Allison! I want to see both of you in my office now," the captain exclaimed, swiping Sadd's last jelly donut before marching through his office door and leaving it ajar for them.

"What do you think he wants to see us about?" Sadd asked Tabitha like things were all good between them.

"I just got here, so how the hell do I know?" she retorted before walking past him into the office.

Sadd shook his head as he followed. He wondered if she filed a complaint on him before she got back to the station.

"Have either of you been talking to reporters, because this case is all over the news?"

"Captain, this isn't our first walk. I can assure you that if there's someone talking to them, it's not us," Sadd answered, stepping in front of Tabitha.

"All of this extra attention surrounding this case is because of the arrest of Noeekwol Bondz. Since he's became an MMA star, the city feels we should be doing more to find his parents' killer or killers and not fucking with him. Now I usually wouldn't give a fuck about none of that, but the chief called and said he wanted an arrest, and for some reason, I promised him we would have someone in cuffs within the next twenty-four hours. So right now I want to hear how you two are going to help me keep that promise."

"Captain, the champ's dad was a low-life piece-of-shit pimp!"

"Yeah, Sadd, but right now all the city sees him as is the parent of the light heavyweight champ who's not getting the attention needed to catch his killer. Detectives, since they're expecting results, I'm expecting results. If you two do not feel you can handle this, then I can find someone who can," the captain threatened, sitting down behind his desk.

"Captain, we're still waiting on a case file from Racine."

"I think we should bring Beysik Bondz in for questioning. The slugs from this case and from the one Allison is talking about are a match, and he's the link between the two," Sadd explained while glancing over at Tabitha and trying to judge her reaction to what he had just done.

"Do you know where he is right now?"

"I don't. But based on the info my partner shared with me, I feel he might be heading back to his parents' home very soon."

"Does that sound right to you, Allison?" the captain asked after noticing the frown she was making as Sadd pitched his idea.

"Yes, sir. I questioned him prior to us having the ballistics report. So it's safe to assume that's where he would be heading since being released from Racine County lockup."

"Why was he in lockup?"

"I put an APB out on him, and they held him there for me to interview him," she explained, trying her best to answer the question and further spark a conversation with the captain about her interview with Beysik so she would not look like she was not being a team player.

"Alright then. Find him and bring him in. I'll have the warrants ready by the time you say it's a go. Now go!"

The captain dismissed them the same way he had dismissed Tabitha's hint.

"Sadd, I want you to be the first to know that when this arrest is done, I'm requesting a new partner," Tabitha said as soon as they were out of the captain's office.

"Allison, wait! Let's just talk like adults first!" Sadd pleaded while watching her ass as she stormed away.

THIRTEEN

Racine County Jail did not have Beysik's release paperwork processed until just before midnight. Beysik was lucky to find someone to accept twenty dollars to give him a ride to the gas station where his car was left parked when he was arrested earlier that evening. Mercy Bondz was forever inclined to suspect the police of doing sneaky things to try to entrap him. This memory of his dad popped into his mind when he made it back to his car. So Beysik instant-aneously removed the battery from his cell phone when he opened the clear plastic bag containing his personal property that had been taken from him upon his arrest. He made plans to buy a new phone as soon as the store opened. But until then Beysik decided to use his tablet to communicate with his girl, Nyte, and the rest of his team via social media.

There was no doubt that Beysik Bondz was his father's son. Through and through, Beysik did his best to be an emotionally in-control individual. But it was hard to be, with all of the craziness that had been happening in his world over the past few weeks. First, there was the mess with his guys being killed inside the Racine brothel because of the two young runaways his dad had sent down to him to put to work.

Now a detective came all the way from Milwaukee just to tell him about his parents' murders. He did not know what to do. He dialed both of his parents' numbers, hoping the detective was just trying to trick him into telling her something about his father. He then tried to reach Noeekwol, whose phone also went straight to voicemail. Beysik then decided just to head to his parents' house to see for himself what was going on. If it was all bad, just like the detective had said, he hoped to find his big brother there so they could decide together where to go from there.

* * *

The harmonic tintinnabulation of Tabitha's phone was annoying. Her soon-to-be ex-partner, Sadd, had gotten in touch with the Federal agent that was heading the investigation of the deceased human trafficker, Mercy Bondz. Sadd easily convinced the gung-ho Fed to join in on the arrest operation to take down who Sadd believed to be the new head of the city's deadly trafficking ring. The phone continued to ring. In a confused fog, Tabitha let it go to voicemail; but as soon as the loud ringing stopped, Sadd called back again.

"What?" she mumbled in a sleepy voice.

"Allison, I got sight on B. Bondz entering the south-side residence of his parents, and I thought you might wanna be here when we go in and arrest that asshole!" Detective Sadd said excitedly.

"Wait! Where are you and who are you with?" she inquired, dragging herself upright in bed. Tabitha instantly noticed that Bret had not come home yet.

"Wake the fuck up! I said I'm outside of Mercy Bondz's residence. I got the Feds to let us team up with them on their surveillance of the place. Do you want to be here when we go in, or not?" he repeated with a slight attitude.

"Yeah. Don't do anything until I get there," she answered, jumping out of her warm lonely bed and rushing into the bathroom to relieve her bladder of the half bottle of Barefoot wine that she drank in anger when she got home from work.

"I thought you might. So I already sent a car to pick you up. It should be there shortly. Allison, if you're not ready when the car gets there, I'm going ahead without you," he informed her before he then ended the call without another word.

Tabitha hurriedly got herself together. She pulled her long strawberry blonde tresses back into a loose french braid and then wrestled on some black fitted jeans and slipped into a pair of black Nike Air Force Ones and a long-sleeved dark blue UW Madison T-shirt. She then grabbed her badge and gun on the way out to an unmarked black Ford SUV that was waiting for her out front of her house.

Tabitha introduced herself to the Federal agent behind the wheel once she was seated inside. Then the agent rushed the detective to meet up with her partner with lights flashing. Once there, the SWAT team that was assembled up the street from the Bondz family home readied themselves for the raid.

"Sadd!" Tabitha exclaimed to get her partner's attention while she walked toward him standing with a small group of police dressed in full riot gear.

"I'm glad you showed up. We are about to storm the place."

"With the Feds?" she asked in a surprised hushed voice.

"Yeah, but we have point on this. All they're interested in is the pimp's personal records of his human trafficking operation. B. Bondz is all ours," he explained joyously.

"Sadd, just for the record, I still don't believe Beysik Bondz had any part in the murders of his parents. With that wise-ass lawyer that his family has on call, this isn't going to end well for us," she said, strapping on her Kevlar police vest.

"I'll be sure to note that in my shift report. Now let's go!"

It was approximately 2:25 a.m. when Detective Sadd gave the order to the tactical officers surrounding the house to move in. Two officers ran up the front porch steps with a black heavy steel battering ram and waited until both detectives were in position behind them. Then they promptly busted down the door.

* * *

Beysik had drank himself to sleep when he made it to his parents' house, so he was on the sofa when he heard the loud, sudden boom that snapped him awake. All he saw were darkly dressed men with assault rifles and riot pumps rush his way. On pure survival instinct and the thought of his murdered parents, Beysik scrambled off of the sofa and made a dash toward the dining room table. He had left his gun there when he arrived and found the place calm.

Detective Sadd spotted Beysik's frantic scamper first and quickly turned his weapon on him.

"Hey, don't move another step! Get down now!" Sadd barked.

Still a little drunk, Beysik made a sudden turn toward the sound of the unfamiliar male voice in the darkness of the house. That's when the detective saw the silhouette of something he believed was a weapon in Beysik's hand, and fired four rapid yet accurate shots in his torso. At that very same moment, Noeekwol came rushing from the bedroom. He was unarmed but ready to defend himself and Heaven from whomever was behind the commotion.

"Police! Get down! Get down now, and place your hands at your side so I can see them!" Tabitha yelled with her gun trained on him.

"Wait! What the fuck is this about?" Noeekwol demanded, complying with the detective's orders.

He then saw his little brother laid out in the middle of the floor fighting to hold on to his life.

"What in the hell did y'all do that for? Beysik! Bey! Beysik, hold on, bro! Hey, one of y'all go get him some help! Do something! Help him!" he begged the SWAT officers that were just standing around.

He was unable to get back up because of the three officers that had quickly pounced on his back.

Tabitha made her way over to her partner who was now standing over Beysik looking a bit distraught.

"Sadd, what's wrong?" she inquired as she followed his stare and saw that Beysik was holding a TV remote control. He was still clutching it while fighting for his life.

"I thought he was about to fire on us. I didn't see what he was holding," Sadd said while looking at her. "Allison, you saw what he did, didn't you? Please tell me you saw what I did?" he pleaded in a shaky hushed voice.

Tabitha said nothing. She only rushed to Beysik's side to try to slow the bleeding until the EMTs were allowed inside of the house. Two medics rushed in and went right to work on getting the wounded man stabilized to transport him to the hospital.

As they worked on him, the SWAT officers zip-tied Noeekwol's hands and then stood him up. Noeekwol heard Detective Sadd tell another officer that they should just let Beysik die. In the champ's extreme agitation, he broke free of the plastic cuffs and charged at Sadd. Noeekwol slugged him with his signature hard, heavy, non-stop violent combination of fists, knees, and elbows.

The shocked officers closest to the detective paused a moment and then snapped into action, tasing Noeekwol twice before he dropped to the floor. By that time, Sadd was bloody and unconscious. The FBI agents placed steel cuffs on him this time and quickly dragged him out of the house.

All Heaven could do was watch helplessly as Beysik was put in the back of an ambulance and race away, while Noeekwol was locked in the back of a black-and-white squad car that raced away in a different direction.

FOURTEEN

After a long week of selling sex and breaking in new recruits for Mercy Bondz's classy underground brothel, Nyte always felt the need to thoroughly scrub each and every inch of herself repeatedly when she got home. Nyte was one of the pimp's high-priced whores, until she fell in love with his son, Beysik, and Beysik with her. So even though working in the brothels disgusted her, Nyte knew it was the price she had to pay for two more months. That was when she would truly be free of Mercy Bondz and could totally be with Beysik and him only, unless he wanted to add to their fun. Nyte liked to be with females from time to time, which is why Mercy Bondz did not want to give her up.

Standing under the hot pulsating water of her home shower, Nyte exhaled as the massaging heat soaked into her tired body. Nyte, who also went by her stage name, Nitemare, was a darker yet shorter version of Tyra Banks, all the way from her wide luminescent brown eyes down to her sexy curvaceous physique. Her looks were another reason it was not easy for the pimp to simply let Beysik have her. His motto always was Money Over Bitches!

Nyte was just exiting the shower when she heard her phone's generic ringtone. She walked dripping naked from the shower to answer it, hoping it was her man calling to explain why he was not at home with her.

"Hello?"

"Nyte, where are you?"

"What?" she retorted, wondering why Heaven was calling her so early in the morning.

"Nyte, I don't know what I'm supposed to do now. The police shot Bey and took Noe to jail, and they won't let me back in the house until they're done searching it."

"Whoa, whoa! Slow down. Did you just say Beysik got shot?"

"Yeah, but they rushed him to the hospital. I don't know which one, and I don't know what else to do. Mama only told me what to do if something happened to her and Pops."

"Where are they at right now while all this is going on at the house?" Nyte asked, pulling on some yoga pants and a T-shirt so she could leave.

"Oh my God! You don't know, do you?" Heaven exclaimed.

"What don't I know? Heaven, what the fuck is going on?" she asked, getting even more frightened.

"Pops and Mama were killed the other night out in front of the house."

"Bitch, that shit ain't funny! Don't fuckin' playin' with me like that! You got my heart beating all fast and shit. I'm about to run outta here half-naked!"

"Why in the fuck does everybody think I'm some goofy bitch that I'd play like this? I'm so fucking serious right now, Nyte. They're dead. Beysik is somewhere fighting for his life, and Noeekwol is in jail!" Heaven explained angrily.

"Oh shit! No! No! No! Let me think. Just let me think. Bey said Mercy keeps a lawyer on the payroll just in case something happens, but I fucking can't think of his damn name right now."

"I know it, and I have his number."

"Okay, call him and tell him to get over there, and explain to him what's going on. I'm gonna call a cab to bring me to you."

"I got the car, so I can come get you. The police told me I can't go back in the house until they're done with the search and fix the front door. So I'm just sitting in the car now."

"Alright, come get me now, then, and call the lawyer. I'ma call around and try to find what hospital they took Bey to."

With the plan set, they ended the call and got on their jobs.

Nyte could not believe any of what she had been told as she took her time and redressed properly. At the same time, she called the county hospital, since she knew it would be the best place to start looking for her man.

* * *

Out of concern for the infuriated champ hurting someone else in his current state of mind, the Milwaukee County Jail's representatives instantly got together and decided that it was best to place Noeekwol directly into the jail's segregation unit. They also had him injected with a mild sedative that calmed him enough so they could safely remove him from the squad car.

Now, approximately thirty-six hours later, Noeekwol was awakened by the tapping of metal on metal.

"Bondz? Hey, Bondz?" a female deputy exclaimed, rapping her keys on the cell door until she saw him move. "Hey, you got court. Get dressed in your oranges and be ready to go by the time I come back to pick up your personal clothing."

"Hey, I ain't even had a chance to use the phone to call my lawyer. So how is y'all taking me to court without allowing me to call him?" he inquired while standing shirtless at the door.

"They may allow you to make a call down in court staging, but I can assure you there will be a lawyer down there waiting to go into court with you. If I remember right, I believe this is just an intake hearing," she explained, letting her eyes wander over Noeekwol's muscular torso.

"Man, I ain't doing shit with a public defender. I need to use the phone now, or I ain't going no-fucking-where!" he barked at her.

"Bondz, please! Let's not do this. I'm telling you that you'll get to use the phone down in court staging. You don't want to upset this judge when he's the one who has to set your bail. Get dressed, please?" She looked over her shoulder. "Because your ride's here," the deputy stated before she then walked away.

Noeekwol conceded and then went over to brush his teeth, wash his tired face, and put on the jail-issued T-shirt, pants, and smock. When the transport deputies came to his cell door to get him, Noeekwol did not give them a hard time about it. He promptly gave them his wrists so they could cuff him before opening the door.

A short time later, he was down in court staging, where he was instantly informed that his lawyer, Jake Sharps, was already in the courtroom waiting for him. Next, Noeekwol was uncuffed but then re-cuffed onto a five-man chain. He and the others were then moved through the back hallways of the jail until they were in the courthouse. The halls were filled with nosey news reporters all with cameras pointed in his face.

Once in the busy, crowded courtroom, an armed, big, black, and bald-headed bailiff walked over and uncuffed them one by one, taking each of the men in orange in front of the judge. Noeekwol spotted his lawyer standing off to the side of the room having a hushed conversation with an all-business-dressed silver-haired female.

It was finally Noeekwol's turn to see the judge. Unlike the others before him, he was not uncuffed completely. Instead, he was only disconnected from the other men with whom he shared the chain. None of the officers or the bailiffs wanted to test their fighting skills against the new light heavyweight champion of the tri-state area. The two courtroom bailiffs escorted him to his spot in front of a distinguished-looking judge, who looked to be in his mid-sixties or so, sitting on the bench.

"I'm glad you're here. They wouldn't let me use the phone or nothing. And they got me in the set unit," Noeekwol hastily explained to Sharps in a low voice.

"Heaven called me right away, so I have an idea of what's going on. I'll come chat with you later. Right now, let's just focus on getting this hearing over with," he told him just as their case was being announced by the court reporter.

"Are you Noeekwol Bondz?" the judge asked with a smirk on his lips.

"Yes, sir!"

"Mr. Bondz, I wouldn't be truthful if I sat up here and pretended like I didn't know who you were. I am a fan, and I hate that we have to meet like this," the judge admitted before he then repositioned himself in his seat. "Mr. Bondz, am I to assume that Mr. Sharps is your lawyer?"

"Yes, sir!"

"Do you understand that you are being charged with first-degree reckless endangerment of the safety of an officer?"

"Yes, sir!"

Noeekwol felt his lawyer nudge his foot so he would not try to explain his actions at this time to the judge.

"Mr. Sharps, have you had time to explain to your client the law of this charge he's facing?"

"Only briefly, Your Honor," Sharps answered.

"Do you need a moment to discuss things further, or do you believe he understands enough to go ahead with things here today?"

"I do believe he understands, and I've already arranged for us to have a visit shortly after this morning's court."

"Okay! Did you explain to Mr. Bondz that the charge he is now facing could change into a homicide charge?"

"Yes, he understands."

"Do we have any updates on the detective's condition?" the judge inquired, turning his attention to the ADA seated at the table beside Noeekwol and Sharps.

The ADA was the same woman Sharps had been talking with before court had started.

"Yes, Your Honor. Detective Morton Sadd is still listed in critical condition, and the doctors are unsure if he will regain consciousness," she answered, now standing at her table.

"Mr. Bondz, do you understand that if the detective's status changes to something more serious, then so will the charge that you're facing now?"

"Yes, sir," Noeekwol answered, fighting the urge to ask about the condition of his unarmed little brother the detective had shot.

"If you were not as well known a man as you are right now, Mr. Bondz, I would think of you as a flight risk. So I'm going to set bail for you today in the amount of $20,000 and place you under GPS monitoring to start at the time the set bail amount is paid. Let's meet back in a week. Mr. Bondz, you are not to leave the city, state, or country while you're out on bail. Do you understand this?"

"Yes, sir. I understand."

"You will be given further conditions of your release upon the set bail being paid in full."

"Thank you, Your Honor," Sharps said before he turned to Noeekwol and muttered, "I'll have the bail paid within the hour. Just sit tight. We will talk once you're home."

Noeekwol agreed and thanked him for being there. When the bailiff came to escort him back to the back of the courtroom for transport, Noeekwol turned his head and saw Heaven and Nyte waving at him from the crowd. All he could do was smile to himself and nod.

FIFTEEN

Noeekwol was wandering around restlessly for about four hours before the set deputy came and informed him that he had a visitor. Noeekwol made himself look as good as he could for the video visit, but he wondered the entire time who could be there to see him.

"Hey, you!" Heaven greeted him when the 26-inch screen blinked to life.

"Hey, what happens now?" he questioned, noticing how aged and tired she looked since they were last really in front of each other.

"Nothing happens, Noe. I just came to pick you up; and since I had to sit here and wait, I just came over to visit you."

"I should be out in a lil' while, I guess. Did they tell you how long you had to wait?" he asked, which released the suspicion from his face.

"Not really. The punk I asked at the check-in desk said it might be taking longer due to them being short-staffed. But he did say you'll be out sometime today. Hopefully before our visit is over with."

"That's how these muthafuckas work. They're quick to lock us up but slow to let us go!" He slowly shook his head in disgust. "I thought I saw Nyte with you. What happened? Where's she at?" he inquired, not seeing her in Heaven's background.

"Oh, I dropped her back off at the hospital so she could sit with Bey and tell him how the funeral went."

"Damn, I can't believe I missed it. Why didn't Auntie hold it off until I got out?"

"We didn't think they was gonna set your bail so low, especially with the dude being the police," she answered, watching the emotion fill his eyes. "Noe, don't get yourself worked up. You know they know you love them and would've been there if you could have."

"I know. How was it though?"

"It was nice. I recorded it, but I couldn't bring my phone over here. They made me put it in a locker, which is just crazy since the visit is on this screen."

"How is Bey doing?"

"He is pulling through good. The doctors say they're keeping him under so he won't injure himself any more than he is already, because there's a lot of swelling around his spine."

"What do you mean, they're keeping him under? Under like in a coma? Heaven?" he pressed her.

"Yeah, he's in a medical coma. They said they can control it, so there are no worries when it comes time to wake him up. They're just trying to make sure he'll still be able to walk when they do wake him up. Nyte has been there on 'em, making sure he is getting the best treatment."

"You know I didn't hear none of 'em in court today say anything about my damn brother. They didn't ask how in the fuck he was doing. But they made sure to ask about the bitch that shot 'im!"

"Noeekwol, don't say nothing on this thing that they can twist up to use against you. You know they're recording this visit so they can try and catch you up in something. Jake said they gotta make you look bad in order to get the people on their side if this turns into a bigger case. So just relax and let's talk about something else."

"Talk about something else, like what? I'm in here, my brother is in the hospital fighting for his life, and I missed my mama and pop's funeral."

Before they went onto the next subject, the deputy came and told Noeekwol to wrap up his visit if he wanted to be released. Noeekwol promptly ended their video call, and about twenty minutes later he was all hooked up on the GPS ankle bracelet.

Somebody told the reporters he was on his way out, so there was a mob waiting to question him outside the front exit. So the transport deputy allowed Noeekwol and Heaven to slip out through the parking garage exit closest to where Heaven was parked on State Street. The two of them made it to the car without being noticed by the paparazzi and sped away from the trying scene.

* * *

Now that Noeekwol was home under GPS supervision, his busy lawyer made a special house call so they could go over their next plans of action in his case.

"I'm going to be honest with you here, Noeekwol. Had you not won that title, you would still be sitting in jail right now. This is a plus for us. It is also a plus that you have not been mentioned, as of yet, in the Feds' investigation of your late father. So we gotta keep the people viewing you as their champ. So please help me do that by staying off of social media and not talking to anyone who could make you look like a common desperate criminal," Sharps said while sitting in a soft La-Z-Boy chair inside Noeekwol's tastefully decorated midtown apartment.

"Which I'm not. I've worked hard to get where I am. I didn't, in a million years, see myself like I am right now."

"I hear you, but you broke a cop's face. That man will never look the same again. You're going to have people that believe that you should have had more self-control than you did when you did that, because you're their champ, Noeekwol. The people can't fairly judge you as a person, only as a fighter who has shown them time and time again his perfect self-control inside of a cage with someone whose only job at that time was to rip your fucking head off. So what you need to do is convince them and me right now that you did not want to do what you did to Detective Sadd. Make me know that you don't hate cops," Sharps told him while picking up his yellow legal pad to jot down some notes, hopefully to use in his client's defense.

"How? I don't know where to start!" Noeekwol confessed.

Heaven saw Noeekwol's desperation fill his face. His vulnerability made her feel the need to protect him from being made to revisit his memories of that night. But it had to be done, and she had to trust Sharps to do his job and save Noeekwol for his and her sake.

"Tell me what you remember about the night of the raid," the lawyer instructed, looking like he was ready to pounce on him.

"Okay."

Noeekwol dropped his head and squeezed his eyes tightly shut for a moment or two. He was doing his best to pull up every bit of the night before he spoke again.

"I was in bed with Heaven that night."

When he said this, he noticed Sharps's smile of approval.

"We didn't even know Bey was in the house until we heard the police kick down the door and start shooting."

"Wait, do you remember if you heard the police announce themselves before the first shot was fired?"

"Nope, they just started shooting. They then yelled 'suspect down, suspect down' after the shooting had stopped."

"Heaven, is that how you remember it as well?" Sharps inquired.

"Yes. I heard someone yell 'gun,' I think, before it started, but it was like at the very same damn time as he was shooting," she explained, happy to be helping.

"Noeekwol, what happened next?" the lawyer asked.

"I ran out to see what was going on, thinking it was the people that had killed my parents. That's when the police caught me by surprise and slammed me to the floor. I didn't try to fight back because I saw they were the police. That's when I saw my brother lying there on the floor, a few feet in front of me, trying to catch his breath. He had blood all over his chest and coming out of his mouth."

Noeekwol closed his eyes again while simultaneously dragging his hand down his face like he was trying to wipe away the picture of his brother fighting to hold on to his life.

"Jake, Beysik didn't have a gun or anything like that nowhere around him either. All I saw was the remote to the TV clutched in his hand."

"So if you were on the ground, how did you attack the detective?"

"They stood me on my feet after they zip-tied my hands. That's when that punk started saying Beysik got what he deserved and was calling him and Pops pieces of shit—and just all kinda shit like that. I snapped. I just snapped and blacked out. I broke the ties and started beating his ass. I don't remember throwing that first punch or how many times I hit him."

"Hmmm! This is good to know. It could be good for us," Sharps said as he glanced at his phone and smiled as he read the screen. "I just got a text from my source at the hospital saying the detective is awake and expected to make it. But he may not be able to work anymore because of the damage to his brain."

"What does that mean?"

"It means we need to make a deal as soon as we can."

"What do you mean, make a deal?" Heaven asked.

"Listen, no matter what or how we put it at trial, Noeekwol, you still beat a cop half to death. If we plea now, the state would be grateful that we didn't drag them through a trial, and they'll be more inclined to give us what we ask for."

"So what do you think we should ask for?" Noeekwol asked.

"To be honest, they're going to want some jail time out of you. But you should not be facing anything more than five years in state prison."

"Five years!"

"That does not mean that you will have to be inside there that long. If you say yes to us plea bargaining, then I will go to the judge we had today and ask him for a set sentence of twenty-four months in and thirty-six months out with earned good time."

"But what about my career as a fighter? I don't know, Jake. I got to really think about this. On top of that, I have to think about more than just myself with Bey in his condition. How come that's not being brought up at all? My brother is in a fucking coma. That's not being talked about at all, and it's because of that son of a bitch!"

"Whoa now, champ! Don't go all Black Lives Matter on me now. I'm on your side. I promise to bring Beysik's condition up when I go in to speak with the judge and ADA. I do believe that would help sway them our way, but you do what you must and think about it. Sleep on it and get back to me. Right now it's a race to see who can get to the judge first," Jake Sharps told them before he got up to leave. "Call me if you have any more questions, or if you need any help getting your affairs together."

"Okay, I will. Thanks!"

Heaven bounced up and escorted the lawyer out. She then came back and dropped herself onto Noeekwol's lap and hugged him.

"Let's not think about that stuff right now. You're already too upset to make that type of decision right now. So let's chill."

"Man."

"Man, nothing, Noe! I told you I'm here for you as long as you want me to be." She kissed the side of his face. "Let me take your mind off of it?" Heaven took his hands and placed them on her breasts and then enchantingly gyrated her hips while pressing her warmth firmly against the erection growing in his jeans.

"Tell me what's on your mind right now. No. Better yet, show me!"

She encouraged him by kissing the corner of his smile before tracing her tongue across his lips until he gave into her.

SIXTEEN

Tabitha made a quick stop home for a change of shoes before she was due in court for Noeekwol Bondz's sentencing. When she pulled up to the house, Bret's car was in the driveway with its trunk wide open. That was an indication to the detective that he did not plan to stay there long. It also made her wonder what he was doing. She double-parked her car and rushed inside the house. That was when she found him boxing up his things.

"Bret? What is this? What are you doing?" she questioned while scanning the room and seeing only his things out of place. "Are you leaving me?"

"Tab! Hon! No, I mean, yeah. Just not the way it looks."

"It looks like you're moving out."

"I am, but I wasn't just going to leave without telling you."

"Bret, I know what I said awhile back about wanting to be married, and I've been meaning for us to talk, but there's just been so much going on."

"No, no! It's not that," Bret said as he set down the armful of shirts he was carrying and took her by the hand.

He led her over to the sofa.

"Tab, I want you to know that I love you, and nothing about this will ever change that."

"Okaaaay, so where are you going with this? What's wrong?"

Bret pulled her down onto the sofa beside him and then briefly took a deep breath and closed his eyes for a moment before he spoke again.

"Tabitha, I'm gay," he admitted as he exhale-ed.

"Gay? No, Bret! What? You? How?" she asked in shock.

"Hon, I just really need to figure me all the way out. All I know is I am tired of running from who I am and how I feel. You deserve better. You don't deserve me lying to you. You don't deserve me cheating on you the way I have been for the past three months. I'm sor—!"

"Bret, are you being serious right now? You're just going to drop this on me like this right now?"

When she jumped to her feet, Bret quickly stood with her, knowing the angry detective was armed.

"Who is this man you're leaving me for? Oh God, what did I do? What the hell! You know what, I don't fucking care! I am glad you're leaving, you fucking lying and cheating asshole! How fucking long?" Tabitha demanded, feeling hurt and crazed.

"How long what, Tab? You're upset, and it's hard to follow what you want to know. Please, just calm down."

"Don't you tell me to calm down! You don't get to tell me shit besides what the fuck I want to know! Now, how long have you been feeling gay?" she asked with a frown as if the word tasted bad.

"I guess I've always had a little attraction to men. I just didn't really know what it meant because I also liked women. It wasn't until a few months ago when Jimmy kissed me and I allowed it. That's when I understood that what I'd been living with you was a lie. I had hoped that the line of work you do would be enough."

"My line of work? Are you telling me you could only fuck me because of my job?"

"No! I, I, I'm trying to tell you that I need to explore this whole other side of me."

"This is a load of crap!" she blurted. "I don't need this shit. I want you out of here by the time I get off work, or I'm going to forget that I am a fucking officer of the law!"

She drew her gun and shoved him as hard as she could with her free hand over the coffee table.

"Arrrggh! So that's where you're going? To move in with this Jimmy guy, Bret?"

"No, no! I found a place of my own. Come on, Tabitha, put the gun away. I'm sorry!" he said, slowly scooting away from her.

"Just be gone when I get back!" she ordered before she turned and stormed out the front door and back to her car.

She let the sirens blast as she raced away.

* * *

Many of the city's news media outlets were in attendance for Noeekwol Bondz's afternoon court appearance. Right in front of the judge's bench were twin tables that were equipped with thin little microphones that swiveled for easy access, and both tables were littered with the current case's files.

At the table on the left stood the defendant, Noeekwol Bondz, along with his shrewd lawyer, Jake Sharps, standing tall right beside him. At the table on the right stood the star female assistant district attorney, Julie Peters, who had been assigned to the case from the start. Beside her was Detective Tabitha Allison, who stood there hanging on every word that was being said by the court officials.

"Am I correct in saying that the defendant, Noeekwol Bondz, wishes to now change his plea from one of not guilty to one of guilty?" the judge asked Attorney Sharps.

"You are correct, Your Honor."

"Is the state in agreement with the defendant's wish to change his plea?"

"Yes, the state agrees, Your Honor," ADA Peters answered.

"Mr. Bondz?" the judge started. He looked Noeekwol in the eyes. "Do you understand that if you change your plea here today, you will give up your right to stand trial?"

"Yes, sir."

"Okay. There are a few more questions I need to ask you before I can move forward today." He shifted some pages in front of him then asked, "Do you understand that I do not have to go along with the time amount offered by the state in the plea agreement, and that I am free to give you more or less than what's stated in the written plea agreement?"

"Yes, sir," Noeekwol answered, starting to second-guess things.

The judge's questions had him a little worried about the deal Sharps had made for him with the ADA for two years in prison and three years out on parole once released. The champ thought of all of the guys in jail with him that he had overheard tell stories about how the judge played them at their sentencing dates. He now wondered if this was what was happening to him with the judge today. He took a shallow breath and told himself to trust in Jake doing his job.

The judge took a moment and sat back in his chair, and continued to look over the papers that his bailiff had handed him from the court reporter. The judge's silence was heavy on everyone in the courtroom. They were all eager to know the fate of the city's champ, and it was stressing the champ out as well.

"I accept that you're making the choice to plead guilty here today under your own free will, and I will allow you to do so," the judge announced after a few long moments. "Is there anything you would like to say to the court before I go ahead with sentencing today?"

"Your Honor, all I would like to do is apologize to the detective's family and this court. I honestly did not mean to hurt anyone in my state of grief that night. It was seeing my baby brother lying covered in his blood right there in front of me that made me black out and snap the way I did. I didn't mean to do it, and I'm deeply sorry for my actions."

"Your Honor, may I add that all of these events came within the week of Mr. Bondz learning that both of his parents had been killed in front of the very same residence where the events of his crime took place in the early morning hours, suddenly and without warning. I ask that this fact be taken into careful consideration, please, sir," Sharps added when Noeekwol had finished his speech.

"Thank you for that bit of information, Mr. Sharps, and thank you as well, Mr. Bondz. Now, Mr. Bondz, I want you to know that I as well as the court understand how a person could lose all self-control after being burdened with so much grief in such a tight timeframe. I do not believe you were in a clear state of mind at the time, and I want you to know that I am taking that fact into consideration."

"Thank you, sir."

"Mr. Bondz, I also do not believe you are someone who thinks that because of his fame he is above the law and expects special treatment from this court. Nor do I believe if given a second chance you would be the type to re-offend, at least not outside of the ring," the judge chuckled along with a few others. "With that said, this court holds you to the same standards of the law as it would anyone else who commits such a crime as yours under those same circumstances, and hereby sentences you, Noeekwol Bondz, to serve eighteen months in the Wisconsin State Prison system and twelve months of extended supervised release. Mr. Bondz, I hope upon your release you continue to be the outstanding citizen and role model our inner-city youth need.

As the judge stood up to leave, Noeekwol asked Jake when he had to start his time, because he would like to see his brother before then if he could.

"Excuse me, Your Honor? We have a question. When does Mr. Bondz's sentence start? He would like to get a few last-minute things taken care of before he has to go in," Sharps asked after halting the judge's exit.

"Oh yes, Mr. Bondz is still out on GPS monitoring, correct?"

"Yes, sir."

"Let me see." The judge looked up at the clock hanging on the wall above the bench and then said, "The time is now 1:45 p.m. Let the record show that I am giving Mr. Bondz until 1:45 tomorrow to report to the Milwaukee County Jail. If he fails to report at that time, it will be considered an escape, and Mr. Bondz, you will be given an additional sentence of up to ten years in prison. Is this understood, Mr. Bondz?"

"Yes, sir. I understand. Thank you, sir."

With everything understood, the bailiff stepped over to Noeekwol's table to escort him and Sharps out into the hallway. Loads of reporters snapped photos and shouted questions inquiring about how he planned on spending his last night of freedom, and how he felt about going to prison. The champ said nothing. He just kept his head down while moving forward away from the courtroom.

"Excuse me, Mr. Bondz?" Tabitha shouted after pushing her way through the mob to talk with him. "I'm Detective Allison, one of the lead detectives assigned to your parents' murder," she explained as she approached.

"Yeah, you're the partner of the dude that shot my brother too. Let's not forget that part," Noeekwol retorted, stopping in his tracks to speak briefly with her. "Do you have something to tell me about my parents' case?"

"No, not at this time, but I want you to know that my job is and always has been to find the ones responsible for it. I intend to continue searching until I have them behind bars. Bondz, I never believed you or your brother had anything to do with your parents' deaths. I am very sorry about what happened to Beysik and hope that neither of you has lost faith in me finding justice for your family."

"Detective, I don't know what you want me to say, besides for you to get outta my face and go do your job. I'm not the one you need to be talking to. You need to be talking to the one that put your partner in the hospital—the one of us Bondz sons that may never walk again. Bye, Detective!" he snapped at her before he marched off with Heaven and Nyte in tow.

SEVENTEEN

The girls and Noeekwol used the time he had before he had to be home for his curfew to go visit Beysik in the hospital. As they approached the nurse's station, the champ was bombarded by fans of his. Nurses and patients asked him for his autograph and to take a selfie. Noeekwol did not mind spending a little time with his fans, especially the nurses, because he knew if he made them happy, they would take even better care of his brother.

"Hey, Brenda! How's he doing? Any changes?" Nyte inquired, when she spotted the head nurse that was also assigned to Beysik's care.

"No changes, but everything's good and steady, which is always a good sign. He's not scheduled for an MRI until morning, so we won't know how he's healing until then," Nurse Brenda answered as she escorted them into Beysik's private room. "Mr. Bondz, my husband and two sons love you. They ask me all the time if I've seen or met you, since your brother is in my care. It would really mean a lot to them and me if I could take a picture with you, please?" she asked, once they were behind closed doors.

"Sure, I can do that. We can take a few."

"I'm sorry I didn't ask when you were just taking them out there with the others, but I'm the one in charge, so I can't let them see me fanning out over you too. Not easy to be able to keep order at the same time," Brenda explained, blushing as she removed her iPhone from her smock pocket.

"It's good. I understand," he responded while looking at the girls standing beside his brother's bed.

When he saw Nyte tenderly holding Beysik's hand, he knew she held real feelings for him, unlike what their heartless father used to tell him about them wanting to be together. Mercy Bondz always told Noeekwol that Beysik was a fool and that Nyte was only using him to get her freedom from the life. He said a hoe could not love anything but a pimp and money.

"Nurse, do you think there's a chance of the doctors waking him up in the morning, because I would really like to talk to him before I gotta go away."

"I really can't say. It all depends on what they see in the X-ray in the morning. I heard what they did to you at court today. I'm sorry that you gotta go through that," Brenda answered sincerely, and then continued, "You should still talk to your brother. Many of the patients that have been placed under a medical-induced coma do say they remember things their loved ones said to them, after they were awakened."

After hearing the nurse's wise words, he put his happy face back on and gave her a few fight poses for her husband and sons. He even had Heaven take one of Brenda holding him in a sleeper choke hold. When they were done fooling around with the selfies, the nurse thanked the champ again and informed him that she would be at the nurse station if they needed her. She then excitedly left the room.

Noeekwol knew, without a doubt, that Brenda was rushing off to forward the photos to her family and post them on her social media pages. He hoped not to hear anything from Jake Sharps about it.

"Noe, I like Brenda, but if these bitches are gonna be hanging all over you like that, then their asses are gonna have to pay. They can fall in line or fall back like the rest of us," Nyte said with a smile.

"Nyte, if I keep them happy, then they'll be good to bro, so chill with all that. Now why don't y'all go somewhere so I can talk to Bey alone."

"Okay, but you only got like twenty minutes left before we gotta go, if you still want to stop for food before you gotta be back at the house," Heaven reminded him before following her friend out of the room.

Noeekwol stood at Beysik's bedside just staring at him and the machine to which he was connected. He just watched the beat of his brother's heart for a long moment before sitting on the edge of the bed. Noeekwol took hold of his hand, which was cooler than he expected it to be. Even though he knew Beysik could not respond, he still filled him in on all that had happened since the night of the shooting.

"Bro, I gave that punk brain damage for shooting you. I tried to beat him to death, but his buddies zapped my ass like three or four times to get me off him. The judge gave me time up north for that shit, so I'ma be gone for a minute. That means you gotta hurry up and get better. I'm putting Nyte and Heaven in charge of the business with your guy Rich's help until you wake up. You know that ain't my lane. That was all you and Pop. I'm having Jake put the house on the market and place the money from it into a trust account for the kids. We don't need that bad-luck muthafucking house in our life. I also had him set it up so the bank will take care of all of the bills so the girls won't have to worry about shit, other than taking care of you and making sure the cash is right. I love you, man. I want you to know that I'ma be expecting you to write me and shit when I get up north, so you hurry up and feel better."

Maybe thirteen minutes later the girls returned, and then Noeekwol and Heaven took off so he would not mess up his curfew. Nyte stayed with her man like she had every night since she found him there.

EIGHTEEN

Tabitha took the rest of the day off from work after attending Noeekwol's court appearance. She was now at home clearing out all Bret had left behind earlier. She did this all while singing along with a recorded live Ani DiFranco concert. Tabitha fast-forwarded the concert along until she came to Ani DiFranco's break up song, "Untouchable Face."

♫ Think I'm going for a walk now,
I feel a little unsteady.
Don't nobody to follow me,
Except maybe you.
I could make you happy, you know,
If you weren't already.
I could do a lot of things,
And I do . . . ♫

Tabitha took a sip of wine right from the bottle of Double Gold French pinot noir which was a gift from one of Bret's friends. Then she tossed a framed photo of her and Bret standing falsely in love aboard a Carnival cruise ship just that past Valentine's Day into a trash box, smashing the frame.

♪ Tell you the truth, I prefer the worst of you,
Too bad you had to have a better half.
She's not my type,
But I think you two are forever.
And I hate to say it,
but you're perfect together.
Fuck you
And your untouchable face.
Fuck you
For existing in the first place . . . ♪

Tabitha heard the doorbell and staggered to open it, already knowing that it was her best friend, Aurora, coming to save her from herself.

♪ And who am I
That I should be vying for your touch?
Who am I?
Bet you can't tell me that much . . . ♪

"Noooo, Tab, I'm not going to let you sit around here and beat yourself up over Bret. I'd always thought he was kinda sweet. From the first time you introduced him to me, I thought he would make you a good wife," Aurora said, trying to make her laugh about her pain.

"Well, I wish you would have said something to me about it then."

"If I did, would you have listened to me?"

"No, I don't know," Tabitha answered sadly.

"No, you wouldn't have! But you are going to hear me now. Tabi, we are not going to do this in here right now. Get your stuff. We're going out to get something to eat and drink. I already made plans to spend the night with you, so we got all night to finish packing his junk and that bottle," she told her after plucking the wine out of Tabitha's hand.

"Okay, let's go. I don't care where as long as I can get a good Long Island, because that wasn't doing the job," Tabitha accepted before pausing the video of the concert.

Out of habit, she grabbed her gun and work wallet before following her friend back out the front door.

The two ended up at Applebee's for dinner and drinks, because it was the closest and served the best Long Island iced tea drinks Aurora could think of outside of them going to a sports bar.

"Excuse me, Detective. Can I speak for a minute?"

"You were with N. Bondz at court today, right?" Tabitha asked, looking up at the woman standing beside their table.

"Yeah, I was. That's kinda what I wanna talk to you about," Nyte said, paying attention to the woman ogling her at the table with the detective.

"Look, miss, I can't do anything about the time the judge gave him. If it means anything to you, I don't believe he should have gotten a day for what he did to my ex-partner."

"Okay! From what you said about still working on finding his parents' killers, I already knew you felt that way. Do you mind if I sit down and talk to you?"

"Only if you don't mind her hearing what it is you gotta say to me."

Nyte looked Aurora up and down and then flashed her a smile before sliding into the cozy corner booth beside her.

"I got something that can help you catch the killers, but you have to keep Beysik and Noeekwol out of it and out of any investigation y'all got going on about them. Because they didn't have anything to do with Mercy Bondz's business. You know what business I'm talking about, right?" Nyte asked her all in one nervous breath.

"Yeah, I believe so," Tabitha responded, not too drunk to pay attention.

"Well, they're not like that, so leave them out and I'll give you something that'll be good for you and get you closer to the muthafuckas who killed Mama and Mercy."

"Miss."

"Nyte. My name is Nyte."

"Nyte, I honestly don't have a case on either of them. I told Mr. Bondz earlier that I don't believe he or his brother had anything to do with the murders, and I meant that. So I can give you my word that I won't try and put a case on either of them as long as they do not have any parts in the shootings. I'm a homicide detective, miss, so that's all I care about."

"That's good enough for me," Nyte said before she then lowered her voice. "Well, you know that Mercy Bondz was into human trafficking."

Nyte paused and dipped her hand inside her Prada bag and retrieved two ID cards. She placed them on the table in front of the detective.

"He got a hold of these two runaways and was breaking them in to work them in one of his spots."

"Are you telling me these two killed the Bondzes?" Tabitha asked, looking at the two young women on the cards.

"No, they didn't. But if you find them, then you might find the people who did. I believe the same people who came and took those two lil' bitches are the same ones who killed them."

The detective quickly took the cards off of the table and stuffed them in her back pocket before promising Nyte again that she would leave the Bondz brothers out of her case. Once assured, Nyte got up and returned to the trick she had left waiting for her at a table across the room.

The information was just what Tabitha needed to keep her mind off of her sudden life change.

"Tabitha, was she just talking about the pimp Mercy Bondz that was killed with his bottom bitch not long ago?" Aurora asked as she flagged over the waitress to refill their drinks.

"Yup, but you know I can't talk to you about my ongoing cases. But if you got something you would like to add?" Tabitha said to her nosey friend before she then downed the rest of her second drink.

NINETEEN

Nyte called Noeekwol before leaving the hospital and suggested that he have a word with the workers in his newly inherited converted apartment building. The building was also home to the family's very lucrative whorehouse, which was just one of several in the state. Nyte wanted Noeekwol to make an appearance at the spot because he was about to go to prison for the next year and a half, and Beysik was in the hospital for however long it would take him to get better.

Nyte knew a Bondz son needed to show his face to ensure everyone understood that she and Heaven only answered to him and Beysik. She also wanted him to prepare them for the much-needed changes that were coming soon.

Since Noeekwol still had a little time to be out on his curfew, he agreed to make a quick stop at the brothel. It was not his first time in the place, just his first time being there without his dad. It kind of surprised him to see how calm business was when he and Heaven walked in. It was Heaven's first time being inside the place of pure prostitution though. Before now, she had only heard of the brothels from Nyte and a few other girls that were allowed to come to Mercy Bondz's home.

As one of Beysik's goons escorted them back to the cash room, Heaven counted maybe ten scantily dressed whores just sitting around talking or wandering around the place. She knew it would not be like this if the pimp was still around, and she guessed they were all curious as to why she and Noeekwol were there.

Heaven was grateful Felisha had saved her from having to work in the place, or one like that, that her husband had owned. While Noeekwol talked to Rich and the other workers about the changes being made and demanded their continuous loyalty during the harsh times, she fought her fear and urge to psych herself up to run and get as far away from all of it as soon as she could. Heaven knew that not spending as much time with the group as Nyte did, it made her less respected and less valuable, especially now that Felisha was dead and her sister had the kids. All Heaven had was the fact that she was fucking Noeekwol, and that was about to be gone. So her future scared her.

Once Noeekwol was sure everyone was on the same page and understood the positions Nyte and Heaven played, he gave them each a $300 bonus to show how much he appreciated them. After issuing out approximately $4,800, Heaven reminded him that he had to rush home to make curfew. It did not go unnoticed that her mood had changed since they were inside the brothel. He saw that Heaven was quiet and stared out the window the whole ride home. Noeekwol wondered what was going through her mind. Up until that point, he had not really thought of her as one of the other working girls the way he did with Nyte. He had just seen her as the nanny. He did not want to force her to talk to him, so he just kept his thoughts to himself and drove them back to his place. Noeekwol just wanted to enjoy his last night of freedom with her stress-free, just the way they had been doing. He needed her to be there for him, and he needed her to keep her word to him. He needed her.

* * *

Tabitha woke up from her Long Island-and-wine-induced slumber at approximately 5:00 a.m. It took her a moment to realize that the warm body lying beside her was not Bret's, but her best friend's. Aurora had stayed over to comfort her, just as she promised she would.

Tabitha's head was foggy from all of the liquor she and Aurora had drunk the night before. Her hangover made her slow to move, but she knew she had to be at the station early today. So she got up and proceeded into the bathroom. She took a hot and then cold shower in an attempt to clear her head for her long day of solving crime ahead of her. Once she was all dressed, Tabitha went over to the bed and lightly shook Aurora by her shoulder.

"Go away! I'm asleep!" Aurora grumbled, burying her head under the covers.

"Hey, listen and you can go back to sleep, I promise," she told her, pulling the covers back from Aurora's face.

"Whhhhhat? I'm listening."

"I'm leaving for work right now. I put the spare key by your phone so you can lock up when you get ready to go. I'll call you when I get a break later, okay?"

"Okay, and you could not have told me all of that in a text, why? Hey, Tabi, is there anything you want or need me to do for you while you're gone?"

"Yeah, if you don't mind doing it. I don't want to see any of Bret's stuff out there in those boxes when I come home. Fuck him!"

"I was going to do that anyway. Tabi, you're better off, and I'm glad you see it or at least are trying to see it," Aurora said with a bright smile. "Don't forget those IDs that girl gave you last night, and tell me if they really do help you with the case. Have a good day fighting crime!"

"Aurora, you're a good friend."

"The best. Now go to work and let me sleep."

The detective snatched up a pillow and hit her friend with it before she ran out of the bedroom. On her way out to her car, she collected her gun and wallet and the two ID cards from the coffee table. Tabitha looked at what remained of her past life with Bret and then kicked one of his boxes and headed to work.

* * *

Unable to sleep for too long, Noeekwol carefully got out of bed, trying not to wake Heaven. He peeled himself away from her warm, soft body. The only thing on his mind in the early morning hour was turning himself in to start serving his time. He only had a few hours before he had to go, and he felt that he needed to be doing something besides sleeping.

"Noe, what are you thinking about that's so good that it made you get away from me?" Heaven inquired as she re-closed the space he made between them and lay on his chest.

"It's nothing good. I just couldn't sleep," he explained, staring up at the ceiling and stroking her arm. "I tried not to wake you up, so go back to sleep."

"I'm up now. Noe, I need you to know that you're way too big to be trying to ease away from somebody." She giggled before she placed soft kisses on his bare chest. "If you need to talk, let's talk. I told you I'm here for you in every way you need me to be," she reminded him.

"I hear you. That's kinda why I can't sleep. I'm not used to this. I don't even know what this is that we got going on here. I mean, we're just nappin', so it makes me wonder."

"It makes you wonder what, Noeekwol?" Heaven demanded, with her thoughts going to their time at the brothel right away.

"Well, damn." He looked down at her then continued, "It makes me wonder what you are gonna do when I'm gone, now that you can do whatever."

"Oh, I wasn't expecting that."

"What was you expecting?"

"Noe, uhmm, I don't know what you wanna call what we got going on, but I know I like you a lot and I'm yours. What part of *yours* don't you understand? Tell me and I'll see if I can help you."

"That part, Heaven," he said as he pushed her off of him so he could see her eyes. "Are you mine the way you were to my pops?"

She hesitated before answering. Heaven never really thought past protecting herself and enjoying being with someone who was with her just for who she was and not for what she did for survival.

"Is that what you want from me?" she asked in her shaky voice.

"What I want from you is truth and loyalty, Heaven. I'm not Beysik or Mr. Big Pimpin' Mercy Bondz. May he rest in peace! I don't get down the way they do. I fight. That's it! That's all! But I'm still my father's son and know how to play the game if I have to. So if you like me, if you're feeling me the way I am you, I need you to promise that you're going to be truthful and loyal to no other muthafucka but me."

"I promise you, Noe, this is your pussy."

"Nawl, Heaven. I want everything. The pussy, the heart, and your mind. I'ma be gone for over a year. I need to know that if you're out here fucking around, that I'm the one you're thinking of. I need to know that when you're fucking, it's not for free. As harsh as that sounds, that's what the fuck I need to know."

"I understand," she said, sitting up with her legs tucked under her on the bed. "Noeekwol, I need you to know that I'm not some weak-ass bitch that you're used to fucking with. A year or two ain't shit for me with somebody I care about. I ain't ever had this in my life. I've always wanted it, but I've never had it until now. Being with you these last few months has shown me that I deserve better than what I've been allowing people to give me. So, yes, I promise all that to you. You have my heart to do with as you please. Just please don't throw it away." She moved closer to the edge of the bed. "Stay here. I got something that can help me prove myself to you right now."

"What is it?"

"Just wait here!"

Heaven got out of bed, tossed on his shirt, and then briskly walked out of the bedroom. She went outside to the Volvo and retrieved her to-go pack that she had hidden in the trunk under the spare tire. Heaven had moved it after Noeekwol had told her he was selling his parents' house, and had given her the car since she liked it so much. Heaven hoped that giving him the money she had stashed would prove to him that she was serious about everything. But just in case it did not, she removed a few rolls of cash and stashed them back behind the spare for safekeeping.

"Here!" she tossed the bag onto the bed. "That's all I got to fall back on if you toss me out. You can have it all, because I want you to trust me the way I'm trusting you with my life right now. Noe, I'm not going anywhere," she vowed.

Noeekwol looked inside the bag and then tossed it back in front of her.

"I don't want your money. You can go put that back where you got it from. I believe that you're mine. Now come here!"

Noeekwol grabbed her hand and snatched her to him. He then kissed her pouty lips. His free hand cupped her arm and he lifted her up off her feet. Heaven locked her shaking legs around his waist and broke their kiss just long enough to pull the shirt over her head.

When her lips found his again, he moved his tender kisses from her lips down her neck. He licked and sucked on her shoulder and collarbone and continuously worked his way down her chest to her breasts. Noeekwol spent equal time with his mouth on her hard nipples.

Heaven pressed her mound against his hardness. The feel of it and his mouth was so exhilarating that she was almost dripping wet. When he felt her body quiver the first time, Noeekwol lifted her up enough to slam her down on his full hardness. The sudden yet explosive pleasurable pain caused her to instantly cum and claw his shoulders, but it did not stop him from roughly bouncing her up and down on his length. She caught his rhythm and began gyrating her hips to make sure he felt every inch of her warmth. Within minutes, they were cumming together while locked in each other's arms. Both felt like they belonged together.

TWENTY

Detective Allison did not have any trouble tracking down the first of the two young women whose ID cards Nyte had given her at the restaurant the previous night. Tabitha just drove to the address listed on the card under the name Lisa Sands. The ambitious detective had high hopes that Lisa would shine a light on the Bondz's murder case by telling her about what had happened to her. If she could get her to do that, it would help close it.

"Ms. Sands, my name is Detective Allison. I'm a homicide detective with the Milwaukee Police Department. The reason I'm here is not that you are in any trouble or anything like that, but I just would like to ask you a few questions."

"Why me?"

"Well, for now, we're talking because your name came up in my investigation," Tabitha explained once she was inside the spotlessly clean and organized home.

"I don't know why. I don't know anything about anything outside of this house. I haven't been a very social person for months," Lisa admitted, sitting down across from the detective at a cozy dining room table.

"What is that?" Tabitha inquired with her pad and pen ready to jot down key notes of their conversation for her records.

"I went through a very personal and tragic event not long ago that made me take a step back from a lot of things and people. I'm sure you know it's crazy out there in the world, and I just need to have a better plan for myself before I get back out there in it."

"Ms. Sands, is it alright if I call you Lisa?"

"Yes, that's fine."

"Okay, well, Lisa, I can understand just what you mean. I've recently made some sudden changes in my crazy world as well," she said to break the ice. "Would you take a look at a few photos for me and tell me if you recognize any of the people in them?"

"They aren't going to be pictures of dead bodies, are they? Because I can't stand the sight of blood."

"No, there's no blood or bodies in these shots, I promise," she assured her before retrieving her phone from her jacket pocket.

Tabitha pulled up the phone's photo gallery and first went to the mugshot of Noeekwol for her to see.

"Do you know this man?" Tabitha asked as she held up the phone so Lisa could see the photo.

"Yeah, that's the dude who won the chance to fight on the UFC's Ultimate Fighter Show or something like that, right?"

"Is that all you know or have to say about him?"

"Yeah, I don't know him personally or nothing, if that's what you are asking. Is he the one that's dead?"

"No, he's very much alive," Tabitha explained before she swapped to the next photo. "Do you know this man?" she asked, this time showing her one of Mercy Bondz's mugshots.

As soon as Lisa saw the face, she tensed up and went pale with fear.

"You know this man, don't you? Lisa, tell me, how do you know him?" Tabitha demanded, restraining herself from badgering her first lead toward maybe solving her case.

"I, I, I think you should go now. I don't wanna talk anymore. If you really need to talk to me, there's going to have to be a lawyer around. I'm sorry. I just can't. I don't want any trouble," Lisa explained, getting to her feet in an emotional stutter.

"Lisa, I promise you if you talk to me now, it can help you. Whatever this man may have done to you in the past, I promise he can't anymore."

"How can you be so sure? You can't promise that!" she exclaimed with tears forming around her light-colored eyes.

"Yes, I can, Lisa. I can promise it because it's his homicide that I'm looking into, so anything that you can tell me can—!"

"So he's dead?" Lisa suddenly asked.

"Yes, and he has been for awhile now."

"How?"

"I'm sorry, Lisa, I can't tell you the details of the case because it's ongoing. But if you can tell me everything you know about him, it would help me get closer to closing this case."

"No! I'm sorry, Detective, but whoever killed that muthafucker did the world justice. I can't help you. I don't want to talk anymore."

Tabitha did not push it. She simply did as Lisa asked, but she made sure to leave her a card just in case she had a change of heart.

After leaving Lisa's house, the detective headed back to the station after stopping and finding the address listed on the ID card for the second young woman, Heather Mosse, up for rent.

* * *

When the time approached for Noeekwol to surrender himself into custody at the Milwaukee County Jail, Jake Sharps was there as requested to escort him inside. Noeekwol and Heaven sat in the rear seat of his lawyer's forest-green Chevy Equinox while he played chauffeur.

Heaven held Noeekwol's hand as he stared out at the freedom that he was about to give up for the next year and a half. When they pulled up and parked in front of the jail, the champ

158

thought of telling the lawyer to pull off and take him anyplace else but there, but he knew his lawyer would not do that. That was the main reason he had asked Jake to escort him today. After getting a few last hugs and kisses from Heaven, Noeekwol allowed the impatient reception deputy to put him in steel handcuffs.

Once again, he was being taken back to the booking room for intake. Just like all of the times the champ had been in this area before, the place was loud and crowded with the scandalous and wasted-looking people of the city. Many of them were guilty, and others not so much, but they all were in for a fight for their freedom—all except for Noeekwol Bondz. He already had his time, and it started the moment he signed himself in at the reception desk.

Since he was a self-surrender, he was fast-tracked through the intake process as soon as the cuffs came off. Noeekwol still went through the whole usual process of being fingerprinted, tagged, and having his photo taken, only without the long wait.

Once he was done in the booking room, he was taken to the back where he was stripped

ASSA RAYMOND BAKER

out of his civilian clothing and dressed in the trusty county orange. Then he was taken up to pod 5-D to await transfer to the Department of Corrections in Waupun, Wisconsin.

On the funky housing unit, Noeekwol got lucky and was placed in a cell by himself. Because he had been brought in late, he missed dinner, so the deputy gave him a cold bag lunch to hold him over until morning. The bagged meal consisted of two mystery meat and butter sandwiches, a small bag of baby carrots, an apple, and a milk. It was a good thing that he ate before he arrived. His aunt had cooked him some buttermilk fried chicken, mixed greens, red beans, and hot water cornbread.

After making the bed, he dropped in it with the bag of carrots and munched on them while lying on the hard, narrow bunk bed. He stared up at the swimsuit photo cutouts of the sexy Kardashian sisters and a few other unknown beautiful models that the man in the cell before him must have plastered onto the bottom of the top bunk to brighten his view.

"Bondz?" the third-shift deputy called out over the intercom.

"Yeah!"

"You're on my transfer list for the morning."

"Alright. Do you know what time?" he asked, now sitting on the edge of the bunk.

"Yeah, I know, but I can't tell you that. You might have one of your crazy fans come and try to break you out if I did that!"

"Ha, ha. Funny!"

"Have a good night," she sang, still laughing at her comment.

Noeekwol got up, took a piss, washed his hands, and then splashed water on his face. He looked in the polished metal that served as a mirror.

"Stay focused. You're all you got, so go in hard and heavy. They can't break you, and they can't beat you!" he told himself, repeating the words of his trainer.

TWENTY - ONE

Detective Allison was sitting behind her desk at work searching for information on the second female's card when she received a call about another multiple homicide. Since she had not been assigned a new partner yet, it was all on her to go investigate it. She quickly left the station and drove to the scene of a witness-reported shooting inside a house on 30th and Michigan Avenue.

When she arrived on the scene, there was a fleet of MPD black-and-white squad cars along with a few other city emergency vehicles parked every which way. All of them were crowded in front of the house. Tabitha wedged her car in where she could and then got out with the last of her Starbucks iced coffee. She downed it and then took a few slow, deep, calming breaths before making her way over to the house.

The detective dropped her empty plastic cup into the green trash bin at the curb and then walked on up the short flight of stairs onto the porch. Stretched out there she found a light-complected male with most of his lower jaw gone from an obvious close-range gunshot to the face.

"Excuse me?" Tabitha exclaimed, flashing her gold shield. "What all do we got on our hands here?" she quizzed one of the two male uniformed officers that were having an unrelated conversation standing beside the body.

"It's a mess, Detective, is all I can tell you," the big guy answered after facing her. "Besides, that poor fella there, there's a few more inside."

He pointed to the wide-open front entrance to the place.

"I really don't know much else. We've been ordered to stand out here and keep the nosey reporters away."

"I'm good with that!" the second officer said before he flashed his light on a guy peeking off of the neighboring porch, who instantly withdrew back inside his home.

"I know how you guys feel. No matter how many times you see this kinda thing, it never gets easier to see. I don't want to be here right now myself. I had only forty-five more minutes to go before I could punch the clock when this call came in. But it's the job that I signed up for," Tabitha said as she inched over to the body lying on the floor of the dirty porch. "Hey, can one of you get a statement from that guy next door? He looked like he may have had something to say," she asked without looking back their way.

She was kneeling down attentively viewing the body of the murdered thug when another officer walked over to her.

"Excuse me, are you Detective Allison?" a female officer inquired.

"Yes, why?" Tabitha retorted, looking up from the corpse.

"They need to see you inside," the officer informed her while trying her best not to look at the bloody mess of a face.

"What do they have in there that cannot wait until I'm done out here?" Tabitha asked, shaking her head at the rookie who was getting paler by the second from the sight in front of her. "Please don't puke all over my crime scene. If you gotta, go over to the curb."

"I'm good," she said as she stood up tall. "It's another male vic. I found him; but unlike that guy, this one's throat's been slashed."

"Alright, then if you're good now, lead the way," Tabitha said as she clicked off her flashlight and followed the officer inside.

The detective immediately clicked back on the light when she stepped inside the gloomy dilapidated interior. It smelled like gunpowder and something sour and very strange. Tabitha was taken to a body slumped over awkwardly in a chair. It was almost decapitated beside a small dirty table.

"Did you find any weapons on him?" she asked while leaning in closer and skimming the beam of her flashlight up and down the victim's arms and hands.

"Weapons?"

"Yes, weapons. The guy on the porch still had his finger on the trigger; and from the looks of this place, it's a drug house. So I'm sure this guy also had a gun on him."

"I didn't touch the body. But I did look all around it, and I did not see anything," the female officer replied.

"Get the team up in here, and tell them to photograph every inch of this room before anything is moved. I'm going to go check out the bodies upstairs if you need me," Tabitha said, heading over to the staircase.

The first thing she observed was the broken banister above and then the bullet-ridden sofa beneath it. She guessed someone had either fallen or jumped down from the second floor.

"Hey, rookie!" she called out. "Tell the team to get shots of all of this area, too, please."

She then continued up the flight of stairs, where she came upon the third body she had seen in the house so far. From what she could see, there was no need for the body shots she saw; and if they came first, then there was no reason for the face shot, unless this murder was personal. She guessed the man laid out in front of her was a target victim.

"Hey, Detective Allison!" the uniformed officer from the porch called to her standing in the middle of the staircase.

"Yeah?" she responded, walking back to the top of it.

"I just got word over the radio that they caught a suspect from here. He's on his way to the hospital. Get this, the guy was T-boned by a speeding fire truck," he explained excitedly.

"That's good to know. Find out where he's being taken. I will come find you when I'm done up here," she told him before she went back to investigate.

She hoped the two were really connected so she could get this case closed fast and get back to the Bondz murders. She needed to give that family some closure, especially after what Sadd had done to them.

TWENTY - TWO

It was roughly 5:45 a.m. when a squad of four transport deputies appeared on 5-D to round up Noeekwol along with sixteen others that were scheduled for transfer to Dodge Correctional Institution that morning. Once Noeekwol was down in court staging for transfer, he was put in handcuffs, blackboxed, and shackled on a chain of five other men. When the deputies had all of their prisoners secured, they marched them down the corridor to a big gray-and-orange prison bus that was idling in the jail's sally port.

Noeekwol estimated about twenty men were already seated on the bus. He found an open seat by the window and sat in it. It did not go unnoticed by him that a few of the men recognized who he was and right away started their whispering about whatever they heard from the news about his case. He did his best to ignore them and not to make eye contact with any of his convicted fans. He was there to do his time, not to make friends, so Noeekwol just stared out of the barred window of the bus.

"Are you really Noeekwol Bondz, the MMA fighter?" the young black kid asked in the seat beside him.

"Yeah, that's me," he responded, not wanting to be rude.

"Dawg, man! I ain't never met nobody famous before!" he said excitedly. "My name's Veteran, but everybody calls me Vet for short. What do they call you?"

"My name is good enough," he responded, still looking out the window at the city as it went from urban to small-town country. "Is that your real name?"

"Nawl, it's my rap name, because I spit fire like the real veterans in the game. I'm known to put that heat to ya feet and leave you hobblin' in pain," Vet answered, showing off his rap skill.

"Alright, now I hear you, but ain't no guns where we're going. So you better know how to use your hands," Noeekwol said, facing the youngster.

"I'm good with these boys, too, but I ain't no Noeekwol Bondz. I used to do a little wrestling when I was in high school."

"Yeah, what happened? Why you stop?"

"I caught a petty weed case and got kicked out of school."

"Is that what you're going up for now?"

"Nawl, I got revoked on my second dirty UA for smoking K-2."

"I see. You didn't get enough of prison the first time, or is it so cool up north that you wanted to come back?"

"Nawl, man, this is my first time going up north. I did time in the HOC for my first bid."

"Vet, man, I'm gonna just sit back and chill for a minute," he told him before he turned back toward the window.

"Alright, man! I'll let you know when we get close, if you're asleep. I'm too fuckin' nervous to go to sleep, but I got you though."

Noeekwol was kind of nervous himself, but he did not let it be known to Vet. Instead, he closed his eyes and reminisced about his last cage fight. He had already proven to everyone that he was ready for the big show in the great octagon of the UFC. He suspected the last match he fought was rigged for him to lose, because they wanted one of the guys out of the Hardball Camp to win it all. That is why he guessed they put him up against the Viking, who had been allowed to drop from heavyweight to fight him in the light heavyweight class. From the Viking's size, Noeekwol knew they were lying about his weight. The man was 230 to 240 pounds easy, but Noeekwol didn't complain. He had never thought his success would come easy. That is why he trained with the big boys.

As soon as he heard the bell ring, Noeekwol dropped his chin the way his dad used to tell him to do when he first started fighting as a kid. With his chin down, he rushed at the Viking to throw him off, while at the same time swinging his heavy hands at full power toward the Viking's head. The two of them had stood in the center of the ring trading blows to the face and head as if they were immune to pain. By the time the bell ended the round, they were both bloody messes. Noeekwol could still remember how glad he was to hear it ring. He went back to his corner wondering if his father was watching him on TV.

When the second round started, he ditched all emotion and went back into his fight mode. This time, Noeekwol did not rush at the Viking; instead, he allowed him to come rush at him. He wanted to make him think he had him intimidated, so the Viking would get overconfident and make a mistake.

Noeekwol went to work chopping the big man down with vicious leg kicks, but he just kept coming. At the time, Noeekwol thought it would be a good idea to change up and go high with his kicks instead of low. But now that he thought back on it, he felt the decision to throw the kick at the Viking's head was just him panicking. He did not know how he was going to be able to put his crazy opponent in such a perfect armbar after he lost his footing and slammed to the floor. But he was glad it popped into his mind when it did, because it gave him the win in the ill-matched fight.

"Aye, champ, wake up. We're pulling up!" Vet informed him, with a slight nudge to his elbow.

"I'm up," he answered, surprised that he had actually dozed off on the bus.

When he opened his eyes, he saw a gloomy monstrous prison sitting firmly behind two double-high electric fences. Both fences were also layered with a multitude of sadistic-looking razor wire at the bottom and top and between the fences.

"Chin down, eyes up!" Noeekwol muttered to himself as the bus pulled to a stop outside the prison gatehouse.

"Everybody get off in a single-file line. Head through those doors where you can see my officers standing. Once you're all inside, you will be given further instructions. Now, is there anybody that has an issue understanding what I just said?" asked the crispy white-shirted captain who boarded the bus to make his announcement.

No one said a word, so everybody was herded off the bus just the way the captain instructed them. Inside the prison, the cuffs and shackles were removed, and the men were broken up into small groups. They were then placed in holding cells until they were called to go through their property. Since Noeekwol did not have anything, he was sent into the shower room where he was put into a stall and strip-searched.

"Take everything off and hand it to me piece by piece," the officer ordered. When Noeekwol was naked, the officer continued. "Open your mouth. Any false teeth or anything I need to know about?" he inquired while looking inside his mouth with a flashlight.

"No, sir."

"Okay, arms up! Let me see your hands." Noeekwol did as he was told. "Turn around, bend over, and spread your cheeks!"

After the demeaning search, Noeekwol was given a strong-scented body wash, and he was told to spread it all over his body from head to toe before the water in the shower stall was turned on. He was next given his state-issued green clothing and a pair of hard brown leather boots to wear. Noeekwol dressed and was marched out and put in line with Vet and the others who were all waiting to have their photos taken and given a prison number and ID card.

"When you hear your name, answer by reciting your number. You must remember that number like you know your name, if you would like to receive any of the services during your stay here at DCI. Again, when you hear your name, answer with your number and line up next to the officer that called you."

"Bondz! Noeekwol Bondz?"

"Here, 00222201!" he answered as he walked over and stood beside the correctional officer.

Noeekwol was glad when he heard his CO call Vet's name. He did not come to make friends, but it felt good to have someone around that he could talk to.

"Hey, champ, they're putting us in the same cell block. I think this line is for the Dungeon in the old building," Vet told him, skipping the men in the line to be next to him.

"Man, go on with that. They don't got a damn dungeon." Noeekwol chuckled.

"Nawl, I'm for real. That's what they call it because the unit is in the basement. My big homie told me about it before I left the HOC.

They put us three to a cell down there, and we can't go nowhere for the two or three days."

"What happens then?"

"I don't know, I guess we get put in GP with the rest of the people here. No homo, champ, but I'm trying to get celled up with you, only because I know you from the bus."

"It's cool, Vet. Man, you good. I was thinking the same shit when I heard the CO call your name. Say, stop calling me champ. Just call me Bondz. I'm trying to keep as low as I can in this bitch. I don't need these people or any of these muthafuckas that think they're tough coming at me."

"Bondz"—Vet lowered his voice—"do you think you can teach me some of that shit?"

For the first time, Noeekwol could see fear in his new friend's face, and he knew he was going to be stuck with him.

"Let's talk about that when we know what's going on with us first, alright?" he told him.

Then the COs headed them all out into the main corridor to be taken to their cell blocks.

TWENTY - THREE

The continuous reverberation of Asad's phones woke up China while he just shifted to a new spot and kept snoring. Irritated by the ringing, China glanced at the time on the clock and guessed that it must be very important. So still half asleep, she reached over Asad and snatched up the cell phone.

"Hello? This better be a real damn emergency with you calling this early."

"Where's Asad, China?"

"Byrd, he's asleep. What's wrong?"

"Wake him up. He needs to go to the hospital right now because Fame got shot."

"Oh God, is he alright? Hold on." She shook Asad awake. "Here, here! It's Byrd. He said your brother got shot," China explained as she clumsily passed him the phone.

"What!" Asad snapped awake and snatched the phone out of her hand. "Byrd, what the fuck happened?" he frantically demanded as he sat up in bed.

"Brenda just called and told me that Fame was brought through the emergency room by the police this morning. She said he got hit by a car and shot. I guess they fucked him up real bad, bro. So you need to get over there before they do some more foul shit to him," Byrd explained.

Asad ended the call and rolled out of bed in a rush to get to his brother. Both he and China rushed around the room gathering clothes and quickly dressing to leave. But Asad was all over the place.

"Bae, I know you're worried, but slow down. It won't do any of us no good if you get hurt trying to get to him."

"I'm good. I just need to find out what the fuck Fame was doing to be shot by the police, and what was his ass was doing out so late for anyway. This shit crazy!" Asad exclaimed while tossing on some ash-gray sweatpants and shoes. "Where is Sky?"

"I'm not sure."

"China, get up with her and make sure she's good. I hope her ass wasn't with bro chasing a few dollars. I'll call you when I find out what's up with him. You let me know if she's good," he said before racing out of the house.

Asad sped through the streets sometimes running stoplights. He had only been out of the house less than ten minutes when his phone started playing the ringtone for Sky. Sky was calling to let him know that she was alright and that she would meet him up at the hospital.

Another ten minutes passed before he was turning onto the grounds of the always busy hospital. Asad quickly found a parking spot and slid the car into it, then jumped out and frantically jogged across the lot right through the hospital's entrance. Asad went up to the nurse behind the information desk and demanded to be pointed in the direction of his brother.

"He was shot by the police last night and brought here like an hour ago, so what you mean you don't got anybody here that's been shot by the damn police?"

"Sir, I've been here at this desk pretty much all night. It's my job to know who's in my ER and why. I'm telling you someone gave you the wrong information; but if you calm down and give me your brother's name again, I can look him up and see if he is here for a different reason for you, okay?" the night nurse explained, standing up from her seat behind the desk. "Sir, your brother is here. He was shot, just not by the police. He is in critical condition right now is all I can tell you at this time."

"What room is he in?"

"I can't give you that information because he was brought in by the police, but if you have a seat in the waiting area, I'll call someone to come speak with you and hopefully answer all of your questions."

Asad agreed and went over to the waiting room. He sat in a seat that gave him the best view of the front desk and the double doors that led back to the emergency room's patient area.

While he waited, he texted Byrd and asked him to call his girl and tell her that he was in the waiting room and they would not tell him anything much. A short time later, Brenda emerged through the double doors and walked up to him.

"Hey, do you know what's going on, because ole girl won't tell me shit. All she said was that she would call somebody to talk to me, and ain't shit happened yet."

"Asad, I don't know much either. The police won't let too many people around him. But I do know he was shot and in a car crash with a fire truck. He's in critical and has lost a lot of blood, but the doctors are working hard to stop the bleeding and get him stable. I'll know more when they're done and come get you to see him if they let me. But I gotta go now," she told him before she then rushed off back through the double doors.

With nothing else to do but wait, Asad turned his attention to the TV and watched a special breaking news report. What really caught his attention about it most was when they talked about a high-speed chase that ended with a car being T-boned by a fire truck.

* * *

Tabitha awoke around ten o'clock and immediately turned on the TV. She then sat up in bed and started checking her emails, just as the overnight breaking news report came on and reported coverage about the Michigan Street homicide case. They were calling it the Michigan

Street Massacre, but that was not why she was upset. The reporter somehow had gotten her hands on information connecting the multi-car accident to her crime scene. They reported that the survivor of the crash was also the number-one suspect in the massacre.

"What the hell!"

"What the hell what, Tabi? Why are you yelling?" Aurora asked, rushing into the room while holding a cup of coffee. "What the hell happened?"

"The damn news just put out info that they had no business having about my case," she answered as she pulled up her captain's number on her phone and called him.

"Wow, that's fucked up!" Aurora retorted while still standing in the doorway.

"Allison, I already know why you're calling, and I'm on it!" the captain said as soon as the call connected. "I've been on the phone since I got in this morning."

"Do you know where they got their information from?" Tabitha inquired, getting out of bed and taking Aurora's coffee from her.

"Not yet, but everybody was told to keep it on the hush-hush last night."

"Well, somebody talked crap, because TMJ 4 is on the air right now with a full report on it."

"I told you I'm on it! Allison, I need you to get a statement from the suspect as soon as you can. Listen, we can talk more when you get in. I gotta go now, so I can get them to pull that story."

"Alright, Cap, but I'm going straight to the hospital so I can question him before he lawyers up on us."

"Handle your business pronto then, Detective," he agreed before he ended the call.

Tabitha dressed in black jeans and a shirt. She then rushed out of the house two and a half hours before she had to report in to work. The detective stopped at a drive-through for a quick ham-and-cheese breakfast bagel and a large coffee. On her way to the hospital, she ate the meal, which made her think of Bret for the first time since their breakup. She hated that she was actually missing him.

TWENTY - FOUR

Noeekwol and Vet made it down to the infamous cellblock known as the Dungeon where they were given their cell assignments. They had not gotten their wishes to be cellies, but they were only a cell away from each other. This meant they would be able to meet up in the chow line. As they wandered through the cell block, Noeekwol looked at all of the faces of the men that stared at them through the narrow rectangular window of the steel faded-gray cell doors.

"Bondz!" a young cocky-looking male CO stopped him. "Put your things on your bunk and come right back out. The security director wants to see you."

"Yeah, alright," Noeekwol acknowledged him before walking into the dull white-and-gray-painted cell.

He examined the insignificant space and was shocked they got away with putting three men in a room that was barely big enough for two.

At the time there was only one other man in the cell. The man looked up to see who had been put in the cell with him, and then pulled his blanket over him and went back to sleep without a word. Noeekwol placed his bedding and paperwork on one of the empty bunks and wondered why Vet could not have been placed in there since there were two open bunks.

"Let's go, Bondz!" the CO shouted from the doorway.

"Do you know what the director wants to see me about?" Noeekwol asked when he finally exited the cell and met up with the officer in the dayroom.

"No, that's above my pay grade." The CO chuckled. "Bondz, you know I follow your career. You're a really good fighter. I'm a fan," the CO said while leading him back out the way he came just a little while ago.

"Thanks!"

"Did you lose your title when you got locked up for this?"

"No, I still got it, because I'll be outta here before I have to start the Ultimate Fighter training camp."

"That's good to hear, man. I'm team Bondz all the way," he said excitedly before he lowered his voice. "I'm Buckley. If you need anything, just let me know, champ, and I'll see what I can do."

Buckley flashed a devious grin just as they were being buzzed through the first heavy security door that led to the control area and the security director.

"Okay, since you say that, can you get my lil' guy moved in the cell with me since there's an open bed in there?"

"Not while you're down in the Dungeon, unless it is for security reasons. But I can see to making that happen for you when you are placed on a permanent housing unit. The Dungeon is just intake. Give me your friend's name, and I'll make a note of it on my to-do list," he said, pulling out his day planner and pen to jot down the name.

"Damn, I don't know his real name, but they call him Veteran. He's in the cell that's one over from mine."

"This is cool. I can find his name easy enough from that," Buckley said before he put his day planner away and then knocked lightly on the security director's door before peeking his head inside.

He informed his superior that he was there with the inmate. After a bunch of "yes sirs," Buckley informed Noeekwol that the director had a sudden meeting and had to postpone their meeting until after the lunch hour and inmate head count.

"So I just walked all the way down here for the hell of it!" Noeekwol complained as he got up from the row of chairs outside the office.

"Yeah, it would have been too much work for her to have called me on the radio and rescheduled. But, Bondz, look at it this way: at least you got some time out of that stuffy-ass cell."

On their return to the cell block, Noeekwol entertained Buckley by answering his inquiries about his life as a fighter. Back in the Dungeon, Noeekwol stopped and glanced inside Vet's cell on his way to his. Vet seemed to him to be in a very heated conversation with the guys in the cell with him. Noeekwol knocked on the window to get his attention, but before they could talk, he was told to keep it moving to his cell by the CO.

This time when he entered the room, Noeekwol's pug-faced chubby Italian cellie was sitting upright on the edge of his bunk fully dressed.

"What up!" Noeekwol greeted him as he crossed the room. He got right to making his bed.

"Hey," his cellie responded dryly. "You might not wanna get too comfortable. They'll be letting us out for chow in a few. Your name's Bondz, right?"

"Yeah," he confirmed, dropping the flat pillow into the pillowcase.

"Do I know you from someplace?"

"You might. I've been all over the TV for one thing or another in the last few months."

"I don't do too much TV watching, so I don't think it's that. The name's Bobby. What do you like to be called?" he asked after extending his hand.

"Bondz, or you can just call me champ. Everyone else is," Noeekwol said while shaking Bobby's hand.

"Why do they call you champ? Do you box or something?"

"You really don't know who I am, do you?"

"Nope."

"How long have you been locked up?" he questioned him, remaining a bit suspicious of Bobby.

"I don't fuckin' know, man. Like three months."

"Oh. Well, I'm an MMA fighter. Does that spark anything for you?"

"Bondz! Bondz! Bondz!" he repeated aloud to himself, thinking on the name. "You're Noeekwol Bondz?" Bobby exclaimed excitedly. "No fucking way. This is you! I lost $300 betting against you about a year ago when you fought Boom Boom Lopez."

"Wow, that was a minute ago. That lil' joker wasn't ready for my weight class," he boasted. "I put his ass down easy."

"Yeah, you did," Bobby agreed, looking alive for the first time since Noeekwol first walked into the cell. "What do you know? I'm locked up with a fuckin' star. Wow! Hey, how did you do in that tournament for the tri-state belt?"

"I took that shit home."

"Oh that's what up. So you got to fight for the chance to fight in the UFC then, right?"

"Yeah, I took it all. You're looking at the new light heavyweight champ," Noeekwol answered proudly right as the door opened for them to go to lunch.

"Man, I wanna hear all about that shit when we get back," Bobby said before hurrying out of the cell.

Noeekwol strolled out behind him at about the same time as Vet was exiting his cell.

"Man, is you good over there?" Noeekwol inquired once he caught up with him.

"Yeah, I'm straight. But let's holla about it at the table. There's too many ears around right now," he answered in a hushed voice as the two of them lined up with the rest of the men from the cell block.

"Alright," Noeekwol responded, now even more concerned with what he had observed when he peeked into Vet's cell.

* * *

Upon walking into the lobby of the hospital, Tabitha immediately browsed through the crowded waiting area. She wanted to see if she could pick out the family members of her suspect. It was a game that she started playing in her head way back when she was a uniformed officer. Whenever Tabitha and her old patrol partner would arrive on the scene of a crime, she would scan the bystanders to see whose emotions were out of place. Most of the time that person would usually know something to do with the case.

However, right now the detective's game was not going the way she wished it to. She wondered if any of the suspect's family members had been contacted about him. Tabitha guessed that no one had been, because when he was brought in, he did not have anything on him that could identify him.

The only words he had spoken before he passed out were, "They're trying to kill me." Tabitha assumed that the "they" the suspect was talking about were the dead men in the mangled car and/or the body that was lying across from him when the police found him in the alley.

But as she approached the information desk, the detective spotted a man sitting with two distraught women, one older and the other about his age. Tabitha just knew they were her people. When she moved a little closer and overheard him explaining a few details about her case and the suspect, it confirmed her suspicions. She decided not to talk to them just yet; instead, she went up to the desk. There Tabitha instructed the hospital staff not to allow the trio back to see her suspect until she had a chance to speak with him first. When everyone agreed, one of the nurses escorted her through the double doors where her suspect was.

TWENTY - FIVE

For third time since he arrived at DCI, Noeekwol found himself being marched down the same long corridor as before. This time he noticed when he passed the doors that led to the control office. He also noticed that many of the officers were lined up outside of their assigned cell blocks to help police the movement through the hallway to the chow hall.

Noeekwol followed everyone down a flight of stairs to the serving line at the end of the staircase. There he received a hard plastic tan tray containing a turkey frank, a bun, diced oven-fried potatoes, a soft lemon cookie, plus one ketchup and mustard packet. He next moved along and was given a choice of a carton of milk or a glass of Kool-Aid. He chose the milk because he did not trust open drinks, nor did he like people reaching over his food or drinks. Lastly, he collected a plastic knife and a spork with which to eat.

When Noeekwol looked up, he spotted Vet just standing there wondering where to sit in the loud, crowded chow hall.

"Let's go sit with my cellie. He's cool," he suggested after spotting Bobby sitting alone at a center back table.

Vet did not care and let Noeekwol lead the way.

"Bobby, want some company?"

"I don't have a choice. Now that y'all here, you can't go to another table or they will trip on you. So you may as well sit down before they tell you to," he explained before he then stuffed his mouth with potatoes.

Noeekwol chose the side of the four-man stainless steel table that put his back toward the wall. Vet sat in the seat that allowed him to keep an eye on his two hostile cellmates while he ate.

"Do one of y'all want the rest of this? I'm just eating the hot dog and drinking the milk," the champ offered, pushing the rest of his tray into the middle of the table.

"I'll take the cookie," Vet quickly spoke up as he snatched it up before Bobby could.

"Sounds good to me," Bobby said, picking up the tray and raking the potatoes onto his tray. "That damn cookie ain't going to keep my belly from touching my back." He laughed before he went back to wolfing down his food.

"Now, Vet, tell me what's up with them fools you in there with."

"Man, champ, I'm straight. It was just that fool with the braids in there was talking some shit. He supposed to be a 1-9 Disciple, and the other punk just wanna be down or some shit."

"So what do that gotta do with you?" Noeekwol asked between bites of his hot dog.

"He's mad because my hood just ran through 19th and sweated 'em before I got locked up. But I wasn't there, so it ain't got shit to do with me."

"What hood you from?" Bobby interjected.

"Brown Street. The ghetto," Vet replied, looking him in the face.

"So you're a Brotha. I'm a King, lil' bro; so if you got drama, I got drama. Just like out there with your hood. If they do something, it has everything to do with you, even if you was around at the time or not. As long as you ain't on no hot shit, we can tear this bitch up, if you wanna tear this bitch up," Bobby exclaimed, flashing quick hand signs to show his loyalty.

"I knew there was a reason I liked you two fools. Both my pops—RIP—and my brother are Lords. I don't bang myself, but I know better than to go against the grain. Vet, if you need me to holla at them fools, I'm there. But like Bobby said, just don't be starting no shit with them," Noeekwol warned his young friend.

"I promise y'all, I ain't on that. Just like you, I'm trying to knock down my lil' time so I can get back out there and on my music shit again. I don't think there's gonna be no mo' shit with dude and the wanna-be. If there was, they would've done something when we were just in the cell."

"Alright," the champ responded before finishing his food and dropping the subject.

About twenty minutes from the time the first man in their cell block had gotten his food and sat down, an officer came over and informed them that chow was over and it was time to get up. Noeekwol and Vet followed Bobby's lead when he went over to the line to leave. They dumped their trays into the trash and then handed them to the inmate dining room worker. The trio used a different set of stairs to exit the chow hall for their return to the Dungeon. Once there, they were once again confined to their cells. Then right after the prison's afternoon standing head count, CO Buckley returned to escort the champ to his meeting with the director.

* * *

Ever since his return from lunch, Vet could sense that something bad was about to happen, so he prepared his mind for a confrontation and stayed ready. He never took off his boots when he returned to the cell. Then at about 1:15, the officer made an announcement.

"Listen up!" he bellowed, standing in the middle of the dayroom to get everyone's attention. "For all of you who have not—let me repeat— for all of you who have not seen the beginning of the Department of Correction's orientation video, when your cell doors pop, come out fully dressed with your shirts tucked in and your boots tied."

Vet sat on the edge of his bunk listening to the direction the officer was giving while staring at his cellmate's feet. Vet was ready for either one of them to make a move on him, even though neither man had said another word since their initial verbal confrontation that took place when he arrived. The tension in the air was thick.

Vet knew to be safe. That was why when he returned to his cell from lunch, he pilfered a plastic knife from the officer's tray and discreetly filed a nice point on it, making it a usable weapon just in case he had to defend himself against his cellies.

Vet had slipped the light shank in his waistband to keep it close at hand.

"Once you come out of your cells, find a seat in one of the chairs in front of the screen and stay there. There will be absolutely no talking. If you are caught talking during the video, you will be given a written warning and sent back to your cell until I decide to replay the video for you again to watch. If you don't complete the orientation video, you will not be moving off my unit. You will not be allowed to go to recreation. Again, come out with shirts tucked, find a seat, and shut up!" the officer said upon concluding his announcement.

He then got on his walkie-talkie and told the control center to open the cells for the video.

When Vet's cell door opened, the Disciple rushed out of the cell first, but his buddy seemed to be procrastinating. Vet instantly assumed that he had already seen the video. Without another thought, Vet got down off of his bunk and headed toward the exit. All of a sudden, the Disciple reappeared with another menacing-looking banger blocking Vet's path. Without giving Vet time to react, the man in the cell behind him suddenly snatched him up into a tight choke hold. Vet tussled to break free of the hold on his neck while absorbing a shower of brutal punches to his face and body by the other assailants.

After receiving a hard knee in his midsection, Vet remembered the weapon in his waistband.

With no second-guessing, he snatched the shank up and plunged it into the thigh of the unknown Disciple, just before another one of the savage knee strikes hit home. The banger howled and jumped back, tripping himself over the stainless steel toilet. On the way down, he banged the back of his head onto the sink before he hit the floor. On instinct, the banger snatched the cruel plastic out of his leg before passing out.

The others saw what happened, and Vet was instantly released by the guy holding him in the choke hold. But Vet was far from free of danger. The remaining guys sent a storm of hard fists crashing into his head and face, knocking Vet to the ground. No sooner than his body hit the floor, did they begin stomping him mercilessly. The two cellies hastily exited the cell, leaving the two unconscious men lying on the floor.

Vet's cellies eased into the crowd that was seated to watch the video, just as one of the officers went around doing a head count before they started the video.

"What the fuck!"

Everyone heard the officer exclaim loudly when she found the two bloody unconscious men lying on the cell floor. She instantly hit the panic button on her radio, and within minutes the cell block was being filled with zero-tolerance correctional officers. They quickly secured the inmates that were in the dayroom by having them all kneel and face the wall, while the remaining officers ran to aid the female who made the call.

After seeing what had happened, a few officers went around checking the men's knuckles in the dayroom for bruising, while at the same time questioning them to try to get the full picture. But everybody out there knew better than to snitch. They did not want to be the next to catch a bloody beating.

To be continued . . .

To order books, please fill out the order form below:
To order films please go to www.good2gofilms.com

Name:_____
Address:_____
City:_____State:_____Zip Code: _____
Phone:_____
Email:_____
Method of Payment: Check   VISA MASTERCARD
Credit Card#:_ _____
Name as it appears on card: _____
Signature: _____

Item Name	Price	Qty	Amount
48 Hours to Die – Silk White	$14.99		
A Hustler's Dream - Ernest Morris	$14.99		
A Hustler's Dream 2 - Ernest Morris	$14.99		
A Thug's Devotion – J. L. Rose and J. M. McMillon	$14.99		
All Eyes on Tommy Gunz – Warren Holloway	$14.99		
Black Reign – Ernest Morris	$14.99		
Bloody Mayhem Down South – Trayvon Jackson	$14.99		
Bloody Mayhem Down South 2 – Trayvon Jackson	$14.99		
Business Is Business – Silk White	$14.99		
Business Is Business 2 – Silk White	$14.99		
Business Is Business 3 – Silk White	$14.99		
Cash In Cash Out – Assa Raymond Baker	$14.99		
Cash In Cash Out 2 - Assa Raymond Baker	$14.99		
Childhood Sweethearts – Jacob Spears	$14.99		
Childhood Sweethearts 2 – Jacob Spears	$14.99		
Childhood Sweethearts 3 - Jacob Spears	$14.99		
Childhood Sweethearts 4 - Jacob Spears	$14.99		
Connected To The Plug – Dwan Marquis Williams	$14.99		
Connected To The Plug 2 – Dwan Marquis Williams	$14.99		
Connected To The Plug 3 – Dwan Williams	$14.99		
Cost of Betrayal – W.C. Holloway	$14.99		
Cost of Betrayal 2 – W.C. Holloway	$14.99		
Deadly Reunion – Ernest Morris	$14.99		
Dream's Life – Assa Raymond Baker	$14.99		
Flipping Numbers – Ernest Morris	$14.99		

Flipping Numbers 2 – Ernest Morris	$14.99		
He Loves Me, He Loves You Not - Mychea	$14.99		
He Loves Me, He Loves You Not 2 - Mychea	$14.99		
He Loves Me, He Loves You Not 3 - Mychea	$14.99		
He Loves Me, He Loves You Not 4 – Mychea	$14.99		
He Loves Me, He Loves You Not 5 – Mychea	$14.99		
Killing Signs – Ernest Morris	$14.99		
Killing Signs 2 – Ernest Morris	$14.99		
Kings of the Block – Dwan Willams	$14.99		
Kings of the Block 2 – Dwan Willams	$14.99		
Lord of My Land – Jay Morrison	$14.99		
Lost and Turned Out – Ernest Morris	$14.99		
Love & Dedication – W.C. Holloway	$14.99		
Love Hates Violence – De'Wayne Maris	$14.99		
Love Hates Violence 2 – De'Wayne Maris	$14.99		
Love Hates Violence 3 – De'Wayne Maris	$14.99		
Love Hates Violence 4 – De'Wayne Maris	$14.99		
Married To Da Streets – Silk White	$14.99		
M.E.R.C. - Make Every Rep Count Health and Fitness	$14.99		
Mercenary In Love – J.L. Rose & J.L. Turner	$14.99		
Money Make Me Cum – Ernest Morris	$14.99		
My Besties – Asia Hill	$14.99		
My Besties 2 – Asia Hill	$14.99		
My Besties 3 – Asia Hill	$14.99		
My Besties 4 – Asia Hill	$14.99		
My Boyfriend's Wife - Mychea	$14.99		
My Boyfriend's Wife 2 – Mychea	$14.99		
My Brothers Envy – J. L. Rose	$14.99		
My Brothers Envy 2 – J. L. Rose	$14.99		
Naughty Housewives – Ernest Morris	$14.99		
Naughty Housewives 2 – Ernest Morris	$14.99		
Naughty Housewives 3 – Ernest Morris	$14.99		
Naughty Housewives 4 – Ernest Morris	$14.99		
Never Be The Same – Silk White	$14.99		
Scarred Faces – Assa Raymond Baker	$14.99		

Scarred Knuckles – Assa Raymond Baker	$14.99		
Shades of Revenge – Assa Raymond Baker	$14.99		
Slumped – Jason Brent	$14.99		
Someone's Gonna Get It – Mychea	$14.99		
Stranded – Silk White	$14.99		
Supreme & Justice – Ernest Morris	$14.99		
Supreme & Justice 2 – Ernest Morris	$14.99		
Supreme & Justice 3 – Ernest Morris	$14.99		
Tears of a Hustler - Silk White	$14.99		
Tears of a Hustler 2 - Silk White	$14.99		
Tears of a Hustler 3 - Silk White	$14.99		
Tears of a Hustler 4- Silk White	$14.99		
Tears of a Hustler 5 – Silk White	$14.99		
Tears of a Hustler 6 – Silk White	$14.99		
The Last Love Letter – Warren Holloway	$14.99		
The Last Love Letter 2 – Warren Holloway	$14.99		
The Panty Ripper - Reality Way	$14.99		
The Panty Ripper 3 – Reality Way	$14.99		
The Solution – Jay Morrison	$14.99		
The Teflon Queen – Silk White	$14.99		
The Teflon Queen 2 – Silk White	$14.99		
The Teflon Queen 3 – Silk White	$14.99		
The Teflon Queen 4 – Silk White	$14.99		
The Teflon Queen 5 – Silk White	$14.99		
The Teflon Queen 6 - Silk White	$14.99		
The Vacation – Silk White	$14.99		
Tied To A Boss - J.L. Rose	$14.99		
Tied To A Boss 2 - J.L. Rose	$14.99		
Tied To A Boss 3 - J.L. Rose	$14.99		
Tied To A Boss 4 - J.L. Rose	$14.99		
Tied To A Boss 5 - J.L. Rose	$14.99		
Time Is Money - Silk White	$14.99		
Tomorrow's Not Promised – Robert Torres	$14.99		
Tomorrow's Not Promised 2 – Robert Torres	$14.99		
Two Mask One Heart – Jacob Spears and Trayvon Jackson	$14.99		
Two Mask One Heart 2 – Jacob Spears and Trayvon Jackson	$14.99		

Two Mask One Heart 3 – Jacob Spears and Trayvon Jackson	$14.99		
Wrong Place Wrong Time – Silk White	$14.99		
Young Goonz – Reality Way	$14.99		
Subtotal:			
Tax:			
Shipping (Free) U.S. Media Mail:			
Total:			

Make Checks Payable To: Good2Go Publishing, 7311 W Glass Lane, Laveen, AZ 85339

CPSIA information can be obtained
at www.ICGtesting.com
Printed in the USA
LVHW011603020720
659594LV00009B/1106